Chesapeake Charlie
and the
BAY BANK
ROBBERS

WILLIAM L. COLEMAN

BETHANY HOUSE PUBLISHERS
MINNEAPOLIS, MINNESOTA 55438
A Division of Bethany Fellowship, Inc.

*Chesapeake Charlie and
the Bay Bank Robbers*
William L. Coleman

Library of Congress Catalog Card Number 80-66638

ISBN 0-87123-113-1

Copyright © 1980
William L. Coleman
All Rights Reserved

Published by Bethany Fellowship, Inc.
6820 Auto Club Road, Minneapolis, Minnesota 55438

Printed in the United States of America

Dedicated to
Jim Coleman

Other Books in this Series

About the Author

William L. Coleman is a graduate of the Washington
Bible College in Washington, D.C., and Grace Theo-
logical Seminary in Winona Lake, Indiana. He has
pastored three churches: a Baptist Church in Mich-
igan, a Mennonite Church in Kansas, and an Evangelical Free Church in Aurora, Nebraska. He is a
Staley Foundation lecturer. The author of seventy-
five magazine articles, his by-line has appeared in
*Christianity Today, Eternity, Good News Broad-
caster, Campus Life, Moody Monthly, Evangelical
Beacon,* and *The Christian Reader.*

Chapter One

It was high enough to make you dizzy. That was what made the train trestle look so inviting to 12-year-old boys. The boney-looking bridge stretched across the green valley and a skinny creek wiggled beneath.

"We have to give it a try," Charlie insisted, leaning against a big gray timber.

That was the way Charlie was. He had to give everything a try. It's easy to understand how he got into trouble with parents, bees, teachers, and dogs.

"I'll get so dizzy I'll throw up all over that thing," Kerry argued.

He was usually willing, but some things made him nervous.

"There's nothing to worry about. The train only comes once a day. Some of the guys have walked across it lots of times." Charlie was pushing.

Kerry squatted on the ground. "I'll sit here and watch."

"Fine with me. When I get back I'll tell everyone I did it and Kerry didn't. Everybody will know you're chicken."

Charlie started climbing up the crossbars. When he reached the top, a disgusted Kerry began shuffling around.

"Grouch! Some people are never happy until they get you killed," Kerry mumbled to himself.

"Wheee. Wheee." The sound was enough to send a dog running under a porch, but Kerry liked it. He made the terrible noise by twisting his mouth to the right and blowing hard. Charlie stopped and looked back. He knew the whistle meant Kerry would be creeping along.

"How long can you stay on a rail?" Charlie was balancing himself on the track with arms spread like a Piper Cub plane. There was a three-foot walkway on each side of the tracks.

Kerry got on the rail and started balancing. You could tell he wasn't happy as he looked straight down.

"It must be a 300-foot drop," Kerry's voice cracked. Actually, it was probably closer to 50 feet, but what difference did that make? Anyone who fell was a sure dead body.

Kerry moved off the rail and began running between the rails on the crossboards. He jumped two at a time. Soon Charlie was doing the same thing.

They felt both foolish and brave. Almost halfway across the trestle they tired and sat on a rail. Each looked at the marsh grass and bushes below.

"Do you think you would ever like to go to sea? Not just the Bay, but an ocean voyage?" Charlie tore a long splinter from one of the boards.

"You mean one of the tuna boats?" Kerry asked.

"Or whatever. The tuna boats at the Wicomico go all around the world. A lot of those sailors don't even speak English." Charlie threw the splinter sidearm, and watched it spin like a helicopter.

"But my dad says there are a lot of dangerous places in the world. You could get kidnapped in India or Russia or some of those places." Kerry leaned back on his elbows to let the sun shine in his face.

"My dad doesn't trust foreigners," Kerry explained.

"Yeah, but it would be different if we were together," Charlie added. "We could watch out for each other. We'd only go for a summer. When we got back we'd have all sorts of stories to tell."

"My dad says there are still pirates near the Asian coasts," Kerry said. "Some boats . . ."

"W-h-o-o-o! W-h-o-o-o!"

The boys stared at each other with eyes as big as baseballs. Surely it couldn't be a train! The second whistle made them leap to their feet.

"Run!" commanded Kerry.

"No time! We'd never make it to the end."

Both knew it was true.

"We gotta' climb down." It was the only thing. Fear grabbed both boys.

Smoke puffed above the trees and a train engine twisted around the corner. The hissing black monster would be on the trestle in seconds.

Without another word they grabbed the side railing and swung themselves over. They had never held anything as tightly as this lumber. They were under the track and clinging to two large round posts with their feet resting on crossboards.

Suddenly the train hit the trestle like thunder. The whole bridge shook as the boys clung for their lives.

"Can anything drip from the train?" Kerry shouted.

"Only if it's carrying acid." Charlie didn't know what he was talking about, but he would never admit it.

Kerry tried to reply, but Charlie could see only his

mouth move; the train was too noisy.

The shaking remained steady and rough. The frightened boys could hold on now, but they wouldn't want it to shake harder.

Finally the green caboose clattered across the tracks. Kerry and Charlie climbed up with their hands still vibrating. Immediately they hurried toward safe ground.

" 'One train a day,' huh? 'Five in the morning one train comes across the trestle.' " Kerry disgustedly clenched his fists.

"That's what the guys told me." Charlie shrugged his shoulders. He was in no mood to be blamed.

"What would you do if they told you nails were candy?" growled Kerry. "Eat a dozen of them?"

It was a quiet walk back to Collin's Landing. Charlie didn't speak but he did feel a little proud. He had beaten the train.

Collin's Landing is a boy's paradise. Girls were allowed to live there, too, but Charlie saw it as his own territory. He liked to visit other places, but the Chesapeake Bay was the most exciting area in the world to him.

Chesapeake Charlie seemed to live for sailboats, tuna ships, water skiing and large crabs. His uncle up in Unionbridge, Maryland, had hung the nickname on him. After hearing him talk so much about the Bay, Uncle George started calling him "Chesapeake Charlie." Now his friends, half of Collin's Landing, and some of his relatives used it too. Charlie didn't mind. He was proud of it and tried to learn as much as he could about the giant waterway which split Maryland in half.

Charlie marched into one of his favorite spots in Collin's Landing—a small general store called "Woody's." It held everything one could pack into a building about the size of a house trailer: fishing nets, a candy counter, boots, a small pickle barrel, and even a counter to sell sandwich meat. Outside was a gas pump which you yourself had to crank—Woody didn't care too much about progress. For his 70 years he still managed to keep up with most things, though.

"Do you still have spark plugs?" Charlie had bought one there a year ago.

"Sure do." Woody liked Charlie. "What size you need?"

"It's for my minibike."

"Are you still riding that? Aren't you kind of big for a Z50?"

"Tell my parents." Charlie rolled his eyes. "They keep saying, 'Next year you can get an XR75.' Next year was two years ago."

While Woody went back to the shelves, a cute girl skipped into the store.

"Hi, Charlie." She smiled.

Charlie tried not to look at her, and mumbled, "Hi, Laura." Charlie felt funny around girls. Once in a while he thought they were nice, but most of the time they were in the way.

"Any crooks in here?" asked Laura with a broad grin.

"Crooks?" Charlie finally looked at her.

"Oh, I forgot you don't have a radio in that creepy shed of yours." Charlie let that pass this time.

"Two men robbed the Easton bank," she continued knowingly. "Roadblocks are north of here, but they might still be in the area."

"How much did they get?"

"Don't know. My parents heard around $3,000."

"With that I'd buy a motorcycle," Charlie snickered.

"Here's your plug," Woody cut in. "It'll be $1.12." Charlie paid and walked outside with Laura scurrying after him.

"Are you going to the regatta Sunday?" Laura treated Charlie as if he were a yo-yo. She wanted to throw him away and draw him in at the same time. "They're racing the log canoes. It'll be a blast."

"Hard to tell. I have a lot of things to do girls don't know anything about."

Charlie cut across the field toward his house. Laura propped her hands on her hips and tightened her lips. She wanted to say something else, but she knew some people are impossible.

When Charlie reached his home he stopped on the back steps. Though he had seen it a thousand times, somehow the beautiful Bay seemed to sparkle in a special way. Large white sails glided across the water while sea gulls arched their wings and pumped themselves higher. Rowboats dotted the shore with silent fishermen waiting lazily for a sudden tug.

It was what his dad called a "postcard day." The skies were bright enough for picture postcards. The deep blue was sharpened by cotton clouds and the winds were just right for excellent sailing.

"I'm home!" Charlie yelled as he banged the screen door behind him. "Hope I'm not late."

The dinner table told him he was just on time. A hot plate of sweet potato biscuits was in the middle and Mother had made oyster fritters. Charlie often felt sorry for people who didn't like seafood. He thought they must surely starve.

When the family was seated, Dad led them in singing, "This Is the Day That the Lord Hath Made." They often did this for their prayer. Then the jabbering started immediately.

"Ya hear about the robbery? Two people were killed." Charlie's eight-year-old brother, Pete, never eased into a converation—he leaped.

"I hear they might be hiding here," he continued.

"Fooey. Nobody got killed," Charlie threw back at him.

"Well, Andy told me he heard it," Pete retorted.

"Andy has chicken liver for brains." Charlie was pouring it on.

"That's enough!" Dad's patience had ended. Mr. Dean knew when to be firm. He managed a canning factory in Easton. "There was a robbery and the crooks got away. But no one was killed, at least not to my knowledge." Mr. Dean summed it up quickly and no one dared to argue.

When dinner was finished Charlie's dad read some verses from the Bible. They discussed them for several minutes and each person prayed. The four were ready for dismissal, but Mrs. Dean had one more subject to bring up.

"Everybody take a piece of paper." She passed a small notebook around. As they each tore out a sheet and stared questioningly at her she handed out pencils.

"Sometimes I feel like we all complain a lot," she continued. " 'I don't like this,' or 'I can't have that.' It gets to be a bad habit. This evening I want each of us to write down just one thing to be thankful for."

You could tell from the boys' faces they weren't thrilled with this new wrinkle. But they knew they weren't being asked, so they got busy.

After a little stewing, each came up with one they thought would pass. Peter was thankful school was out, and Charlie was grateful for his new tape player. Dad wrote down, "a loving wife and mother," while Mrs. Dean remembered her healthy and happy family.

The four things weren't amazing or complicated, but this activity helped them to remember how much they each depended on the Lord and on each other.

Everyone was dismissed with slight smiles on their faces. Each person had to carry his dishes to the kitchen. This was a family rule at the Dean home. Sometimes the boys were embarrassed when eating at their friends' homes, because they often forgot and picked up the dishes there. But, still, it was a good way to help at home.

Everyone heard Kerry thump up the back steps and call, "Charlie!"

"We're going to ride the bike, Dad," Charlie announced as he moved toward the door.

"Fine. I bought you some gas. It's in the trunk of the Chevy," replied Dad, as he tossed over the keys.

Chesapeake Charlie snatched the keys and was gone. Pete didn't even bother to ask if he could ride, too. Sometimes Charlie let him, but never when a friend was over.

They had a large backyard next to the water. Five acres was small when they got the minibike out; however, it seemed huge when they had to mow the grass.

The bike was soon gassed up and running. Their spotted dog, Throckmorton, jumped at the noise. He was a friendly beagle they had owned for five years.

Charlie plopped down on the minibike. He looked as if he were wearing his knees for ear muffs since his legs were so long. He wore his helmet obediently, though he hated the thing.

Their circular track had only one small bit of excitement. On the farthest corner from the house was a slight mound. When they hit it just right, the squatty vehicle would leave the ground and fly for just a second. They had hit this spot so often the minibike had developed a few rattles.

"Let's do something different." Charlie, like a lighthouse, was always searching. "I've thought of a great picture."

"Picture?" Kerry was cautious.

"I was thinking. Mom has this roll of paper she uses to cover the picnic table. We could hold it up and crash through it just like the commercials."

"And take a picture as the person crashes through," added Kerry.

"You catch on fast," said Charlie.

"There is only one problem. How can you hold up the paper and take the picture at the same time? You aren't going to ask Pete, are you?"

"No, there has to be a better way," Charlie reassured.

"We could make a wooden frame to hold the paper," Kerry piped in.

"You do come up with a winner once in a while."

Both boys headed for the garage.

Within half an hour they had nailed four two-by-fours together and added legs to hold it up. It was about five feet tall and soon white paper was stretched across the frame and nailed into place. In a minute Charlie had scooped up the camera from his bedroom and dashed outside with Throckmorton bounding next to him.

Both agreed one thing was missing. The white paper needed decoration. Taking paint from the garage they drew a large green circle on the open space. Two more circles turned it into a target.

After it was set up on the track Charlie handed Kerry the camera. Kerry handed it back. Charlie handed Kerry the camera. Kerry handed it back. They had one more problem. Who would get to ride through the green and white wall?

Just when it looked as if the fantastic flying bike might never take off, a surprise poked its head around the tool shed. The surprise had brown eyes, a short haircut and blue jeans. "Laura!" the boys cried. They'd never sounded so friendly to her. Never.

"You're both crazy," was her immediate response.

"C'mon give it a try," urged Charlie.

"It'll make a great picture," chirped Kerry.

"Can't you see it in the newspaper: 'Photo by Laura Phillips,' " Charlie encouraged as he smiled at Laura for maybe the first time.

"It'll look dumb." Laura tried to hold her ground but she was weakening.

"No, it won't. We'll build a ramp and sail through the air," explained Charlie. "We can use two cinder blocks and put . . . put . . . Dad's spare tire on them. I've got a board for the ramp."

Kerry looked surprised about the ramp but started talking anyway. "And Charlie and me are going to ride double!"

"We are?" Charlie was wide-eyed.

"The only fair way," nodded Kerry.

"You two tubs will break the bike. But maybe that'll be a good flick." Laura was being sarcastic. "I can see the headlines now. 'Two Clowns Collapse at Collin's Landing.' " The boys would put up with her jokes if she would merely take the picture.

Soon the blocks were collected and the spare tire removed from the trunk. The two-foot-wide board promised plenty of ramp.

Helmets were quickly donned, the motor was sputtering, and Charlie and Kerry straddled the bike like state troopers—eyes fixed straight ahead, necks stiff like plaster casts, and Charlie revving the engine like a cross-country champion.

Laura crouched into position on the other side of the target. She would count to three and they would head around the track. Just as the paper burst she would catch the picture and hope to become famous.

"One!" Laura shouted, holding her arm high.

Charlie revved the engine.

"Two!"

Kerry pushed his helmet down tighter.

Laura dropped her arm. "Three!"

The minibike jerked and lurched forward. Throckmorton yapped and began chasing the bike. They turned the first corner of the track and picked up speed on the straightaway.

The target was only 100 feet away and in spite of the weight of the two boys, the bike was moving well.

Charlie had to swerve around the dirt mound before hitting the specially built ramp. His front tire clipped the edge of the mound and the bike jumped to one side, almost throwing Kerry off. Kerry grabbed at Charlie, inadvertently wrapping his hands around the driver's eyes.

Kerry couldn't straighten up and Charlie couldn't see. Throckmorton raced alongside, barking in excitement.

The beagle and bike arrived at the target at the same time. The minibike missed altogether and Throckmorton, his eye on the boys, bounded through the paper just as Laura clicked the shutter.

Charlie and Kerry veered past the target, sending three geese scurrying as the bike splattered into the shallow water. Both boys fell off.

Kerry lifted his hands full of chocolate-fudge mud as Charlie spit out a short stream of water. They stared at each other in bewilderment.

Laura came running, laughing so hard she could hardly get her breath. Throckmorton cocked his head to the left and looked confused.

Chapter Two

Charlie didn't like to work around the house. He would run errands or clean his room, but only when he had to—and when his mother could find him. However, when it came to catching dinner, Chesapeake Charlie was always glad to help.

"Let's have crabs tonight," his mother announced.

"I'll catch them!" Charlie didn't even have to be asked.

He bounded outside to the back porch and collected equipment: a long-handled net, a few lines, and some pieces of raw chicken necks.

"Charlie!" The yell sounded familiar. Kerry was back.

"I'm only three feet away from you," grunted Charlie. "Want to go crabbing?"

"I don't know. I'm still mad at you about yesterday. Mom says you're a reckless driver," Kerry declared.

"*I'm* a reckless driver? Who grabbed my eyes?"

"It was your fault for jerking the cycle. My mom said—"

"Would you like to go crabbing or not?" interrupted Charlie.

"Well, I guess. But remember, you're dangerous. That train trestle almost got me killed."

"You take the bucket, I'll get the net," ordered Charlie.

"My mom said—"

"The chicken's in the bucket." Charlie tried to ignore him but it wasn't easy.

Charlie liked crabs; the funny little creatures had two claws that could give you a sharp pinch and their tiny eyes stuck out like they were on the ends of sticks. The oddest thing about crabs is the way they walk: instead of straight ahead, they scoot sideways. But that doesn't slow them down. If one gets on dry land, he can move like a spinning top to get away.

"Had any bites yet?" Kerry was getting anxious. His legs were hanging over the dock, bare feet dangling a foot above the water.

"Just a few nibbles. Mostly it's minnows trying to get some free chicken."

"Let 'em visit the Colonel—not us," joked Kerry.

"I think I've got something! Get the net," commanded Charlie.

Crabs can be easy to catch if you handle them right. Something was chewing on the chicken, so Charlie eased his line toward the surface. The crab kept eating.

"Hold it steady. I see him." Kerry whispered hoarsely and moved to Charlie's side, dipping the net swiftly into the water under the bait and hungry crab. Kerry swung up and snagged both into his net and out of the water.

"I've got it! I've got it!" Kerry yelled.

It was a good-sized crab. They had to be five inches across the shell in order to keep them, and this one was probably seven.

Kerry turned the net upside down over their water bucket. The crab had pinched the net strings and didn't want to let go, so Kerry beat the net on the bucket and tried to shake it loose. He had to be careful or the crab would fall on the wooden dock and get away.

"Let go, big guy," Charlie told the crab.

Kerry smacked the bucket one more time and the crab fell "plunk" into the water. It raced around but there was no way out.

"Got ya!" exclaimed Kerry defiantly.

A dozen or so of those, and the Dean family would have a tasty meal. Charlie had put six lines into the water and would check each in turn. If he or Kerry felt something pull on a line, they would bring it in.

The sea gulls were beautiful today as they soared around the dock like kites. Sometimes it looked as if they were hanging in the sky without moving at all.

Charlie threw a piece of chicken skin a few feet away. A gull swung down, snatched up the foot, and took off, without hitting the water.

Out on the water they could see gulls following a large motor boat. The motor stirred up the water, causing minnows to come to the top, and sea gulls would scoop down and steal supper.

"Got one!" Kerry declared.

"Got one," Charlie echoed.

So the afternoon went. Sometimes they would get several bites in a row and the next ten minutes might be quiet and uneventful.

"One more and we can call it quits," Charlie announced.

"I think I've got a nibble," Kerry responded.

Chesapeake Charlie picked up the net and ran to Kerry's side. Carefully the bait was pulled in and the net slipped into place. The crab was hauled onto the dock, and Charlie swung toward the bucket and turned the net over. It was a beautiful blue crab with full, red-tipped claws. It dropped and hit the side of the bucket, tumbling onto the dock.

"He's loose!" cried Kerry.

"Don't let him get away!" shouted Charlie.

The frisky creature moved directly toward Kerry's bare feet, making the boy dance like popcorn.

"Get him!" Kerry was desperate.

Charlie took a swat at the crab but missed. Kerry stomped his bare feet to frighten the crab, but it kept charging him. Kerry jumped in the air and screamed. Charlie took another swing at the racing crab but missed.

As Kerry came down, his legs were spread wide open, his feet barely clinging to the edge of the dock. The crab ran between Kerry's legs and tumbled into the water. Charlie was chasing so fast he couldn't stop and piled into Kerry, the net going through his legs.

Kerry grabbed at Charlie with both arms in a bear hug and for a moment they tottered on the edge of the dock trying to gain their balance. A second later they collapsed, sending Kerry backwards, yelling, into the water with Chesapeake Charlie on top of him. Fortunately, the water was only three feet deep, but the water splashed as if a plane had crashed.

"Ouch! Ouch!" howled Kerry. "It's got me. The crab got my foot!"

"Grab my hand." Charlie helped Kerry to his feet.

"To the shore, the shore!" Kerry was dancing high.

In a minute both boys were on shore. Kerry sat on the first log he saw and held his left foot.

"Look at this cut." Kerry pointed to his big toe.

Charlie examined it with great care.

"Looks like you nicked it on a stone." Charlie gave no sympathy.

"What do *you* know? I was attacked by a wild crab and you call it a stone! You're the reason I went into the water to begin with. My mom says you're going to get me killed some day."

"It's only a scratch, Kerry."

"I bet that isn't what my doctor will say." Kerry limped away.

At home Mrs. Dean took out the large black kettle. She had steamed crabs so many times the process was almost automatic to her. She poured three cups of vinegar into the pot and added the spices: four tablespoons of salt, four tablespoons of dry mustard, four teaspoons of black pepper, and one teaspoon of red pepper. Her mother had always added tabasco but Mrs. Dean's family didn't care for it.

When the mixture started boiling the crabs were dropped in, kicking vigorously. They would be steamed for 20 minutes while their color would change from dull green to a brilliant red. The red color meant they were thoroughly steamed.

"Make sure our car and house are locked tonight," said Mr. Dean as they sat down at the table. "Those bank robbers haven't been caught yet."

"They wouldn't still be in the area, would they, Dad?" asked Charlie.

"Maybe they have kidnapped a family," added Pete.

"You're always so funny," retorted Charlie, sarcastically.

"There is nothing to worry about," Mrs. Dean

reassured as she began to open a crab shell. "But there is no sense in being foolish either."

Each member of the family had a kitchen knife to open the crabs. The blade was used to open the shell and get to the spicy meat while the handle became a hammer to crack the claws. The claws held large pieces of juicy meat.

"Watch out for the dead man's fingers, Pete," warned Mr. Dean.

Dead man's fingers (really lungs) were eight, or so, feathery-looking pieces. No one in the family was sure how they could hurt you—maybe make you sick or kill you or something. The Dean grandparents had warned the parents, and now the parents warned Charlie and Pete, so the boys would probably tell their children the same thing: "Don't eat them."

The crab meat had a rich taste which went well with a cold glass of iced tea and crackers. It was fun to take your time eating, visiting and picking at Mrs. Dean's green salad.

"I met a visitor today," said Mr. Dean. "I think his name is Hagan. He comes from Vermont—a state trooper there. He rented Mrs. Higgin's cottage for a week. He must be six foot two or three, and he likes to fish and crab."

"From Vermont?" Charlie chimed in. "Then he can't know much about the Bay. I'll have to go over and fill him in."

As they finished dessert, Mr. Dean reached for his Bible on the bookshelf behind him. Charlie and Pete stopped their chattering as their father flipped open the Living Bible and began to read from 1 Timothy.

Charlie's mind started trailing off to catching

crabs, but Mr. Dean's voice was too loud for day-dreaming.

"For the love of money is the first step toward all kinds of sin. Some people have even turned away from God because of their love for it, and as a result have pierced themselves with many sorrows. Oh, Timothy, you are God's man. Run from all these evil things and work instead at what is right and good, learning to trust him and love others, and to be patient and gentle."

Pete was trying to be very serious. "Those bank robbers sure must love money pretty bad, huh, Dad?"

"They certainly must, Pete, if they had to rob for it. But, these verses aren't just about bank robbers. We all have to watch our attitudes, because God wants us to be content with food and clothing—whether we have anything else or not."

Charlie gulped. "Does that mean I'm not supposed to want a new minibike?"

"Not at all, Charlie," his mother assured. "God wants us to have desires, as long they're not desires for wrong things—and if you're content to wait for God to provide it. If He wants you to have that bike, He'll give it in *His* time. But, if love of money—or a new minibike—makes one jump the gun and disobey God, it seems one always ends up in a mess."

Charlie drooped down in his chair. He certainly didn't want to disobey God, but that new minibike seemed awfully far away at the moment.

After they finished praying, Charlie and his dad

carried the crab shells out back to the garbage cans. Cleaning up was easy if they carefully folded the newspapers Mrs. Dean had spread on the table.

"What's that flag?" Charlie asked his father.

A large tuna boat was gliding past their home heading north. Its gray bow sat high in the water making the two-hundred-foot-long vessel look like the queen of the seas.

"I believe it's Spain," replied Mr. Dean. "They seem to be bringing more loads into the Bay this year."

"Must be heading for Baltimore," said Charlie.

"It's hard to say. It could be going to Cambridge; not many of them go to Salisbury anymore."

"Why not?" asked Charlie.

"They're getting too big for the Wicomico River. Those big ships need almost forty feet of water to navigate safely."

"Did you ever want to go to sea?" Charlie continued.

"Sure, when I was your age I dreamed about it all the time. Your uncle and I would sit on the bank and watch the boats and try to guess which country they came from. We got pretty good at it. But now—at my age—I'm happier with a motor boat."

"Not me," added Charlie. "Someday I'm going to sail to India or Persia or Australia."

"You never know, son. Maybe you'll even become a ship captain."

Charlie decided to find the state trooper and introduce him to the many wonders of the Bay. Whatever problems Chesapeake Charlie had, being bashful wasn't one of them. He would probably be willing to shake hands with an alligator.

"Hi! I'm Charlie Dean. Everybody calls me Chesapeake Charlie."

The trooper stood up from the net he was repairing. He was so tall he seemed to unfold rather than stand, and his smile was as wide as a boat bow.

"Sounds like a good name to me. I'm Kent Hagan. Why do they call you Chesapeake Charlie?"

"My uncle made it up. I guess it's because I enjoy the Bay so much. There's a lot to do here."

"I can see that," said Kent.

"Looks like you're going crabbin'. The best time is early in the morning or else when the tide's in."

"This is my first try at it," volunteered Kent. "Somebody told me to tie chicken on a line. Will that work?"

"As well as anything," said Charlie. "Some people go at it big and set out traps. They use plastic milk jugs for floats to mark where they sink the traps. Some people even use eels for bait."

"You seem to know a lot about it all right."

"While you're here, you should watch the crab boats do it professionally. They sure bring in the crabs," added Charlie.

"My wife isn't sure she wants to go crabbing. She's afraid of those claws," chuckled Kent. By now he had returned to repairing the torn net.

"She'd probably like to visit the historical sites. There are plenty around the Bay. There are lots of pirate stories. There might even be sunken treasure in the middle. It's over 100 feet deep in some places."

Charlie was in his glory whenever he could corner a

newcomer and begin pouring it on. Kent was patient, but he was also interested.

"One good place to take her is St. Michael's. It's a neat little town. Women like the shops."

"We might try it."

"But that's not the best part. St. Michael's has a fascinating history. It's the town that fooled the British. Have you heard the story?"

"I'm afraid not."

"Good." Charlie was almost jumping for joy. It was one he loved to tell.

"During the Revolutionary War the British tried to control the Bay. They sent ships through the area to wipe out the Americans—or whatever we were called then.

"When they came to a town their ship would sit in the harbor and lob cannon balls into it. Most of the towns were helpless against the big guns.

"Some men in the area saw a gigantic British ship plowing through the Bay heading for St. Michael's. The people didn't know whether to fight or run.

"Since it was getting dark, someone suggested a better plan. They quickly carried lanterns outside town and hung them in the trees. When the British ship came, it stopped offshore from the lights. They cranked up their big guns and blasted away. When most of the lights were blown out they figured they had destroyed the town and pushed on. Actually they didn't even dent St. Michael's. People around here have been talking about it for 200 years."

"So I see," said Kent, "and it's a great story to tell. We'll have to visit the town."

"That's only part of it. Have you heard about the

pirate who had five skulls tied to his mast?"

The trooper knew he was in for a long session.

Two men moved quietly behind the white rowboat parked in Charlie's backyard. They kept their heads low and stepped carefully.

"I still don't like the idea." Ben Patterson hadn't shaved for a couple of days and his eyes were red from lack of sleep. "We can't hide the money here."

"Will you shut up," Fred hissed at him. "The whole area is crawling with cops." His gold front tooth sparkled each time he opened his mouth. "We can't get caught with the money. We'll get a motel room, and after things settle down we come back, pick up the dough, and head for Florida."

"I still don't like it," said Ben.

"What are you, a broken record?" Fred's eyes halted on a white, overturned bait box.

"What if someone finds the money?" argued Ben.

"No chance," explained Fred. "No one has opened this bait box for years. I'll put the money in it and just turn it back over on its lid next to this rock. In two days we come back and take off."

"We better not get caught." Fred's eyes searched around like a submarine's periscope. "Let's beat it."

"You're too nervous, Benny, my boy. We'll get movin', but first, I'm starvin'. You see those donuts on the porch? What say we grab a couple."

"You must be crazy." Ben sounded desperate as he grabbed Fred's shirt.

"Don't be so yellow." Fred pushed him back and started to skulk toward the Dean back porch. Crouching low, he darted from the boat to a nearby tree. Ben remained behind the eight-foot vessel, not sure exactly what to do.

It had been over 24 hours since the two crooks had eaten, and Fred could practically taste the donuts. When he got close he saw two tall glasses of cold milk in the center of the table.

Suddenly Mrs. Dean appeared on the porch with another glass of milk and put it down. Fred dropped to the ground close to the house. Mrs. Dean couldn't see him and merely turned and went back into the kitchen.

One sound would give this robber away, but for some reason he loved to take a chance. As quietly as a flea tiptoeing on cotton, he opened the screen door and stepped inside. He could hear Mrs. Dean and Pete talking. Quickly he stuffed six donuts into his shirt and grabbed one glass of milk. He was gone like a whisper.

Pete wandered onto the porch, missing Fred by thin seconds. He heard a noise in the bushes. Pete looked. He stared. There was nothing, so he picked up a donut and walked back into the house.

Fred rejoined Ben and started chuckling. His greatest thrills were cheating and stealing.

"Here, take a couple donuts. You stick with me, my shy friend, and I'll teach you all sorts of things."

Still drinking his milk, Fred and Ben disappeared into the trees.

"I've often thought of becoming a state trooper when I grow up." Charlie had been telling his stories for over two hours now. "I think I can handle a crook. If he gives me a hard time I wouldn't hesitate to shoot."

Kent Hagan had opened two bottles of pop.

"A lot of people have the wrong concept of a trooper. Our main job is to help people, not to hurt them.

"Sure, I carry a revolver, but in eight years I've used it only twice."

"Only twice?" Charlie was shocked.

"That's a high percentage. Most troopers don't fire that often."

"Not even twice?" He couldn't believe his ears.

"The first time was when I had been a trooper only one month. A man had a pistol at a highway rest area. When I approached him he took a shot at me."

"Did you kill him?" Charlie was wide-eyed.

"No, I shot back but missed. He was so frightened he dropped his pistol."

Charlie was clearly disappointed.

"What about the second time?"

"That was different. Four years ago I got a call about a robbery in progress. It was in a small town less than a mile from where I was cruising. When I arrived the robber had just come out of the bank. He turned to take a shot at me and I fired. It got him in the shoulder."

"Just a nick, huh?"

"Don't let those nicks fool you, Charlie. It wrecked his shoulder. He'll never be able to use it properly again."

"Whatever happened to him?" asked Charlie.

"Last I heard he was serving 15 years. But, again, that isn't our real job. Television shows make a big deal of that part. Most of the time we just help people.

"If someone speeds we pull him over—not to hurt him but to protect him and the other people on the road."

"How would you like to tangle with those crooks from Easton?" asked Charlie.

"I don't know what you're talking about. I stay away from newspapers or radios during my vacation."

Chapter Three

The screen door squeaked open and gave a sudden bang. There stood Chesapeake Charlie, grinning from ear to ear. Woody and Laura were sitting in the general store by the old black stove.

"I bet I know something you don't know," he blurted out as he grabbed a third chair and sat down.

Woody and Laura were hesitant to ask what, but they knew they had to.

"I'll bite," ventured Woody. "What is it?"

"Some crabs are poisonous." Charlie held his chin high.

"Thanks for nothing." Laura sounded disgusted. "You mean they can bite you and you'll die?"

"They are poisonous," continued Charlie.

"You're nutty," declared Laura. "How come nobody in the Bay dies from crab bites?"

"There *are* poisonous crabs!" Charlie had Laura baffled and he was thoroughly enjoying the tease.

"Your brain is poisonous!" Laura answered.

"Tell us about it, Charlie," joined Woody. "What do you mean by poisonous?"

"Well, they don't really kill you by biting. But if you eat certain crabs, their meat could kill you." Charlie's smile stretched like a tight sock.

"You mean if I eat a certain crab, it will kill me? You're gross." Laura was completely bewildered.

"What you say may be true, Charlie," said Woody. Laura's face twisted. "But maybe you still have some more to tell us. Are these poisonous crabs in the Bay?"

"Well, maybe. I'm not saying," replied Charlie.

"It's all a big story you made up," charged Laura.

"That's what you think," Charlie retorted.

"Come on, Charlie. You could at least tell us where they live," suggested Woody.

"Some of them are as close as Hawaii," stated Charlie.

"Four thousand miles away? You're shaking me up about a crab that lives on the other side of the world?" Laura was perturbed. She would never understand 12-year-old boys and wasn't sure she wanted to try.

"Some of them live in the Red Sea, and Africa, and even Japan," added Charlie. "People die from them."

"You are correct, Charlie." Woody was always kind. "There are a few species which are poisonous to eat. But none around here. There are over 4,000 different kinds of crabs in the world."

"That many?" Laura was surprised.

"Of course some are small enough to hide in an oyster shell," continued Woody. "Others weigh up to twelve pounds."

"I want to go see the new crab farm," added Laura. "They're raising soft shell crabs for sale."

"It sounds like a great idea if it works," said Woody. "We could feed even more people if we use the Bay correctly. By raising crabs we should be able to produce even more food."

"Well, I have to run. My dad is going to take us to the baseball game this evening," announced Charlie.

"Kerry is going to go with us to see the Detroit Tigers play Baltimore." He glanced at Laura and teased, "Glad I could add to your knowledge about crabs."

Charlie slammed the screen door behind him and went whistling down the road. He was glad Woody wasn't a bossy man because the store was always a good place to stop.

Kerry was waiting when Charlie arrived home. He loved baseball and even brought his glove along. If there was any chance to catch a foul ball, he was going to be ready.

"It'll be an hour before we leave," Kerry told Charlie. "Any chance of some food?" Kerry was hungry only twice a day: when he was awake and when he was asleep. He even dreamed of food.

"Let's see what we can dig up," agreed Charlie.

On the back porch there were two tables where Mrs. Dean often stored food. It was a good hunting ground for hungry boys.

"Both of you go away," ordered Mrs. Dean as she walked onto the porch. "You have already stolen my donuts and milk."

"Your what?" asked Charlie. Puzzled, he glanced at Kerry and shrugged.

"You heard me. Now both of you run along. Dinner is almost ready."

As they started out the door Charlie spotted a pan of oysters so he grabbed a couple and kept moving.

"I've got a terrific idea," Charlie told Kerry. "Have you ever eaten a raw oyster?" He held up the two shells he had taken.

"Not me," responded Kerry. "My uncle eats those

things raw. They look sick."

"I don't blame you for not eating one. There aren't many of us who can eat them raw." He paused. "It takes extra courage to do it."

Kerry clearly didn't like the suggestion that he was chicken. Charlie pulled out his pocket knife and opened the blade.

"Laura will understand when I tell her *I* ate one and you didn't."

Kerry didn't like that either. He was sure he didn't like girls, but he hated to look like a coward in front of one. Charlie started to tear at his oyster shell.

"Who knows. It might even have a pearl in it." Charlie was acting brave and superior.

"Quit it," insisted Kerry. "If you can eat one, I can." He drew his own pocket knife and took the second oyster. He began prying at the shell.

Charlie's oyster opened first and he started to poke around with his blade. He had once found a tiny, lopsided pearl and always hoped for a big one.

"Let's see you eat yours first," challenged Charlie.

"No thanks," replied Kerry.

"You aren't going to eat your oyster, are you?" asked Charlie.

"Of course I am." Kerry wasn't really so sure. "I've eaten them before." But he couldn't remember when.

"Well, go ahead," egged Charlie.

"You go ahead."

"I knew you weren't going to do it," added Charlie.

"I've got a better idea. Let's count to three and swallow them together," suggested Kerry.

Charlie agreed.

"Do you chew yours or just swallow it?" asked Kerry.

"Well, swallow it, of course," answered Charlie. By now he wasn't too sure he could eat it either way, and the more he looked at the oyster the funnier he felt. The glands just under his jaws started feeling strange—like they were filling up.

"One," went Kerry.

"Two."

"Three."

Both boys turned their shells upside down and gobbled their oyster off into their mouths. They were slimier than either had remembered. It was like trying to swallow raw liver.

In a second both oysters were down—hopefully to stay. Kerry and Charlie looked at each other with wobbly smiles.

"Not too bad," announced Charlie. He barely got the three words out. Then he grabbed his mouth and turned his head. Charlie made the awfullest noise anyone had ever heard, as his oyster and everything else in his stomach shot out like an open fire hydrant.

Charlie was embarrassed. "I must have had a bad oyster," he said feebly, continuing to spit.

"Sure Charlie—I understand. Wait till I tell Laura this," teased Kerry.

"Let's go to the shed," said Charlie. He was disgusted but he knew he would think of something.

"The oyster was your idea, Charlie." Kerry stopped walking.

"Well, it must have been a rotten one," Charlie insisted.

"I have an idea of how you can get even." Kerry was feeling victorious and his brain was turning. "Go in the house and bring me two uncooked eggs."

"That sounds great." Charlie's voice was perky.

"You should see me balance eggs."

In a minute Charlie was back, carrying an egg in each hand.

"Watch this." Charlie put one egg on his forehead and started to balance it.

"Not so fast." Kerry clearly had the advantage over Charlie and he knew it. "That's not what I had in mind."

"Well, you name it, ole Kerry. I can do anything with an egg you can. Want to balance it on your finger? How about the top of your head?"

"Anything?" asked Kerry, his eyes gleaming like light bulbs.

"You name it, Kerry. How about on your foot?"

"Okay, but before we get started, let's make sure I understand. You will do anything with that egg I will. Correct?"

"You've got it!"

In one grand motion Kerry lifted his egg to face level and shoved it into his mouth. Without hesitating Kerry crouched down and started chewing it, shell and all. After five or six chews he swallowed everything.

Charlie gasped. He just stared in disbelief. What was Kerry, a trash-masher?

"I can't eat that," whined Charlie. "Only crocodiles eat raw eggs. Besides they might have little parasites that make you sick."

"That's terrific," Kerry replied smuggly. "Laura will be glad to hear this too!"

Charlie looked at the egg like a sad puppy. Sometime, somehow, he would get Kerry for this.

"We'd better move, boys." Mr. Dean was eager to

get going. At least a couple of times a year he tried to get to a baseball game. It was no easy trip to Baltimore, but he thought it was worth it. The downtown ride on Charles Street frustrated him, but it was the only way.

Mrs. Dean, Pete, Kerry, and Charlie piled into the green Dodge and they were on their way. Mr. Dean had mailed away for special box seats along the third-base line.

The best way to Baltimore was across the Chesapeake Bay Bridge. The traffic was often heavy and a second bridge had been built. Mrs. Dean said the traffic seemed just as congested with two. Both bridges gave a beautiful view of the Bay and its ships.

"Mom, I looked it up in the encyclopedia and the bridge is four and a half miles long." Pete was proud of this information. People were always arguing over the length of the bridges.

"One more time, Pete, so pay attention." Charlie couldn't keep out of the conversation. "The bridges are seven and a half miles long, so throw your kiddie encyclopedia away."

The three boys were sitting in the back seat, with Kerry in the middle. The thirty-minute ride to the bridge was usually lively with debate.

"Who is right, Dad?" asked Pete.

"For once, both of you are. The bridge itself is four and a half miles long over the water. If you measure from where it starts and finishes on the ground, it is seven and a half miles."

"How high is it?" asked Kerry.

"I think I read 186 feet above the water at its highest," replied Mr. Dean.

"Wow!" exclaimed Pete.

Pete tried to make the most of trips. Sometimes he would try to get trucks to honk at him and at other times he made signs to show to other drivers.

"Honk, honk," sounded the car behind them, startling Mr. Dean. When Pete laughed out loud, his father smiled good-naturedly, realizing what had happened.

Pete had some old signs left from one of their longer trips. He merely held them up to see what kind of response he would get. This one said, "Honk if you like Donald Duck." Drivers would give a gigantic grin and honk away.

He had other signs that were just as fun. "Donate to your local worm farm" was a big winner. So was, "Did your parents have children?" The signs helped to pass the time and sometimes Charlie even joined in. They seemed to cheer up the many drivers who read them.

It was early evening but the traffic was already beginning to back up at the bridge. People from Washington, Baltimore, and all over crossed the bridges to go back and forth to the Eastern Shore and Ocean City. Often cars were backed up two or three miles waiting to get on the bridge. Sometimes more.

This evening the Dean family was behind almost two miles of cars going slowly. This bridge was three lanes wide and carried cars from east to west. The other bridge had two lanes and traffic moved west to east. On the west shore there were toll gates, and each car had to pay $1.25 for using the bridge.

Mr. Dean hoped he had left early enough to catch the ball game. He was sure he had, but he never knew what might happen. The traffic moved in spurts. One minute it would jam tight and the next it would open up for 100 yards.

Just as their car moved onto the bridge everything opened up and the vehicles started flowing.

Some visitors have trouble looking down on the water, but those who are used to it enjoy the thrilling sight. Travelers are soon up on the same level as sea gulls, while majestic sailboats glide underneath. Huge ocean vessels plow their way toward the Baltimore harbor.

In a few minutes the Dean car was at the exciting top of the bridge. The boys strained their necks to see the ships below.

"Whop-de-whop-de-whop."

"What's that?" asked Charlie.

Mr. Dean knew instantly what it was. He had a flat tire and it couldn't have picked a worse place to collapse. Cars were whizzing past him at fifty miles an hour as he carefully pulled over to the right.

"I'll have to change it," said Mr. Dean disgustedly.

It was definitely a dangerous thing to do because the lanes weren't wide; but it had to be done. The car halted safely by the curb and Mr. Dean jumped out. He quickly opened the trunk to gather his jack and spare as cars surrounded him.

Traffic was slowing down considerably because the Deans were blocking one lane and hindering a second. A few of the people who passed them even yelled embarrassing remarks.

Mr. Dean suddenly climbed back into the front seat. He whirled and stared hard at the three boys.

"Where is my spare tire?"

Charlie and Kerry could remember. It flashed through their minds for one horrible second, like a nightmare. The spare was still under their ramp. The boys said nothing, but Charlie thought how valuable vanishing cream would be right now.

Rap—Rap—Rap.

Mr. Dean turned to face his left window. A large blue-uniformed policeman glared down at the car. Mr. Dean lowered the window like a schoolboy about to get chewed out.

"Hurry up, Mister. You have to change that tire and move it."

Mr. Dean edged himself out of the car.

"I'm afraid I don't have a spare, officer."

"You what? You mean to tell me you came on this bridge without a spare? Some people! I'll have to call a wrecker and have you pulled off. Get back in the car."

Horns honked and people yelled as they pulled out and went around the Dean car.

Mr. Dean sank down in the driver's seat, too upset to say anything. Raindrops started falling on his windshield.

Chapter Four

Charlie didn't have much to say the next morning. Mr. Dean assured Charlie the next morning that he was forgiven, but he would lose his allowance that month. As he left for work, though, he was still a little disgusted about the tire. Charlie ambled out into the backyard just to poke around. Kerry probably wouldn't be over this morning; he was afraid Mr. Dean would scalp him.

Charlie couldn't be more confused. "Some days it seems like the whole sky falls in," he thought as he walked slowly to the waterfront. Throckmorton followed him and Charlie patted the old beagle on the head.

He looked at the beagle and smiled. "Mom thinks this mutt is the greatest watchdog in the world. The truth is he wouldn't chase a cat, let alone a burglar."

Charlie sat on a log by some bushes and brushed Throckmorton's ears.

"Dogs probably are man's best friend," he said out loud. "Girls certainly aren't friends. Sometimes even parents don't understand you."

Throckmorton blinked at him.

"I bet you don't know who stole the most bases in one season, do ya? Lou Brock stole 118 bases in 1974. You don't know who had the most walks in one year. Babe Ruth walked 170 times in 1924.

"Dogs and girls. Neither of you understand base-ball."

With one disgusted thrust Charlie kicked a white wooden bait box in front of him. It flipped over twice and the lid flew open. Pieces of green paper tumbled out.

Charlie's eyes caught them immediately but couldn't quite comprehend what he saw. In three large bounds Charlie was at the box. He bent down and picked up a piece of paper and looked it over.

It was the size of a dollar bill and had a picture of Andrew Jackson on it. In each of the four corners was a number 20. Charlie looked in the box and there were more pictures of Jackson—over a hundred pieces.

"Twenty dollar bills!"

He dug a little deeper into the box and found $50 and $100 bills.

"Man, there must be thousands of dollars!"

He thought for a second, then quickly stuffed the bills back into the box and slammed the lid.

"Now shush, Throckmorton. We can't tell anyone about this money. Not until we've thought this through."

The beagle merely turned his head to the right and wagged his tail.

"This money could belong to a rich widow. But we can't be sure of that. It might belong to a wealthy hobo. Sure! He was traveling through here and left it in this box and he wants us to have it. You and me, Throckmorton.

"Of course, we would share it with Mom and Dad, a little. Maybe a twenty for Pete.

"That's it! A wealthy hobo left it and now it's ours.

We can't prove that, but no one can prove a hobo didn't leave it.

"I know what you're thinking. You think this money belongs to the Easton bank, don't you? Well you're wrong, Throckmorton. You're wrong. That's all. What do you know? You're just a beagle."

Throckmorton looked up with his dark eyes and tilted his head.

"Until we know what to do we had better make sure the money is safe. We don't want any crooks robbing us of our inheritance.

"We can't keep it in the house or Pete might find it. Let's build a safety trap and leave it here. Throckmorton, you guard the money while I get some equipment."

Charlie left for the house while Throckmorton lay down and closed his eyes.

In a few minutes Charlie returned with an armful of materials. Continuously checking to see if any people were coming, he started to make the box burglarproof.

First he drove large nails through the lid of the box, leaving the pointed ends sticking up. Then he glued it shut.

His third step was the most important. He tied three small bells to the back of the box. If anyone dared touch it Charlie would be out of the house and on them in a flash.

Then he put the box behind a heavy growth of weeds. Even if the money wasn't his, no one could blame him for guarding it. Besides, he had heard that if no one claimed money in 30 days, it went to the finder. At any rate the box could sit while Chesapeake

Charlie thought it all over.

And he had the best protection of all: Charlie would leave Throckmorton on guard.

Laura had warned Charlie she was going to come over some morning and make him go crabbing with her. Today was the day. She always claimed girls could catch crabs better than boys because girls had a more sensitive touch on the line. Charlie always dismissed this with a typical, "Nuts," but had accepted the challenge.

"Charlie, Charlie!" she squealed.

He came out of the weeds immediately, half afraid she had seen him with the white box.

"I've come to beat you. One hour of crabbing and the one with the most wins."

"Not today, Laura; now beat it."

"Afraid as usual. I'll stay here and make noise until you agree to go."

"See if I care," replied Chesapeake Charlie.

"What a big bluff you turned out to be," said Laura.

"All right, I'll beat you," answered Charlie, as he clambered into the rowboat. "But let's only go out a little way." He wanted to keep an eye on the spot where the box was hidden and listen for the bell.

"You use chicken and I'll use eel," said Laura. "I think chicken fits you better!"

Charlie was furious but didn't say anything. "She'll change her tune when she finds out I'm rich," he thought.

"I don't know why I should do the rowing. I thought girls were better than boys," Charlie said sarcastically.

"Girls *can* do anything." Laura always had a reply. "But gentlemen know how to be polite. Since girls are pretty they deserve to be waited on."

"Maybe if you were pretty I wouldn't mind waiting on you," retorted Charlie.

Laura tried to stare a hole through Charlie.

He hadn't rowed far when Charlie pulled in the oars.

"Well, this is far enough for me," said Charlie.

"You mark the spot, I catch the crabs," remarked Laura.

While they prepared their lines they could see jellyfish pushing past the boat. These soft, slimy creatures aren't jelly and they aren't fish. Their tops are round like nearly transparent umbrellas. They have string-like arms called tentacles which hang loose in the water. Small stingers (like tiny springs) line each tentacle.

The jellyfish, sometimes called sea nettles, have almost no power of their own. They swim a little by pushing their bodies but usually follow the waves and current.

They catch their dinner by stinging it and then lifting it up into their heads. The jellyfish don't seriously hurt humans but can leave nasty stings and create welts on the skin.

"I've got a bite!" screamed Charlie. He held the line with one hand and slowly moved the net into position with the other. In a quiet scoop he swung the net under and brought up the crab. A good-sized one, it was snapping and clawing all the way into the bucket.

"That's three, Miss Fisherman. Do you still have your skinny one?"

"I'm not the least bit concerned. We have 20 minutes to go. The bigger crabs are waiting to get on last."

"Ha! Ha! Ha!" When Charlie wanted to, he could have the most insulting laugh.

The final 20 minutes were agonizing for Laura. She caught one more crab, but Charlie pulled in two more. With only a few minutes left, the count was 5 to 2.

"Ha! Ha! Ha!" He laughed so hard the boat rocked.

Now Laura was steaming. She threw herself over the side and stood nearly waist deep in the water.

"Don't tell me you're quitting," said Charlie.

"You know," she retorted, "you can be disgusting."

Laura reached over, took a large jellyfish by the head, and in one fast motion hurled it out of the water at Charlie.

"Aaaaaah!"

Charlie leaped back but the long tentacles smeared against both of his bare legs. He threw the oozy monster back into the Bay.

"You're a rotten loser, Laura!"

The words were wasted as Laura walked steadily toward the shore, her head high.

"I'll get even with you for this!" Charlie shouted again.

Charlie was busy scooping water and splashing it on his leg. Despite his frantic work it was too late. The stingers had struck. Painful bumps started rising on his skin. Like little red bee stings they appeared in small groups.

When Charlie got back to shore the stinging had grown worse. He grabbed a handful of mud from the soft ground and spread it on his wounds.

This was one score he would have to settle with Laura—and not in the too distant future. His mind was already starting to cook up a plot.

As soon as Charlie got to the house and had spread some medicine on his wounds, he was off to Woody's general store. The bumps had gone away by now and all that remained was the embarrassment he felt.

Charlie brightened up the minute he walked into the store. The only customer was Trooper Kent Hagan. Charlie liked him.

Hagan greeted him with a grin, "Hi, Chesapeake. What you up to?"

"Nothing much, Trooper." Charlie was proud just to know a policeman. "Did you go fishing this morning?"

"A little while, but didn't catch anything. I'm going to get some salted eel and see if the crabs are hungry."

Charlie was burning to ask him a question but felt he better not. He wasn't quite sure how he was going to handle the money. If he told someone, he was afraid he would lose it.

"Have you ever visited the FBI building in Washington?" Charlie decided to avoid the money problem.

"Can't say I have. I bet it's interesting." Kent knew he was in for a description.

"Man, do they have a fascinating gun display. I forget how many rifles and pistols they have. At the end of the tour a special agent does some marksman shooting. He used a handgun and a Thompson submachine gun the day I was there."

"They are good shots all right," added Kent.

"I bet you troopers have to work closely with the FBI."

"Sometimes they come in handy."

"They said they can get all kinds of information just from a single hair." Charlie enjoyed talking. "They can tell what part of the body a hair came from. They can tell if it has been dyed. They even know how it came off the body—whether it was cut, pulled, or even fell out by itself. I bet they could find out just about anything they wanted to."

"Well, pretty close," admitted Kent.

"Sometimes I think about becoming an FBI agent. You have to go to law school or become an accountant first. I think I'd become a lawyer and then an agent. I'd put in for special assignment around the Bay."

"Why not? You could do it if you tried," said Kent. "Well, I got my eel. Come on over sometime and we can fish together."

"I will," replied Charlie. "But right now I have some pretty important things to take care of. Maybe later."

The trooper left the store and Charlie turned to Woody who stood behind the counter.

"Do you have a few minutes, Woody?"

"Now, time I have. I don't have much energy and very little money. But I have 24 hours each and every day. Let's open a couple of sodas and just sit."

Woody's cooler was a tub filled with ice covered by a metal lid. Nothing fancy but it got the job done.

"My friend—you don't know him—has a real problem. I told him I would get your opinion on how to solve it."

"Well, I'm not Sherlock Holmes but I'd like to listen."

"It seems my friend found some money. He won't say how much it is. Probably $15 or $20. So far he doesn't know where it came from and now he doesn't know what to do with it."

"You mean he is wondering whether to turn it in or keep it?" Woody tried to sum it up.

"That's about the size of it."

"Where did he find it?"

"He won't tell me," Charlie continued. "But it might have just showed up in his yard. I'm just guessing at that. He never has told me."

Woody knew there was more to this than Charlie was telling. He decided to ask a few more questions without getting pushy.

"Has he tried to find the real owner?" Woody asked.

"Well, not yet, but I'm sure he intends to. So far he doesn't know where to ask."

"He could begin by checking with his neighbors. Just ask if anyone has lost any money. Don't tell them how much and see if they can identify it," added Woody.

"But suppose, just suppose he already knew it didn't belong to his neighbors?" wondered Charlie.

"Then the next step is to check with the police."

Charlie choked on his soda.

"You better drink that a little slower," cautioned Woody.

"I guess I—I mean he hadn't thought of the police. Is it true that after 30 days you can keep it?" Charlie asked.

"I don't really know about that. I do know a person should attempt to find the owner. If he keeps it quiet, like hiding it, it's really like stealing the money."

Charlie put his soda bottle down; he didn't want to choke again.

By now Charlie was sorry he had asked. He knew the money hadn't fallen out of heaven or grown from under a rock. It had to belong to someone. Charlie fought the facts. Maybe, just maybe . . . he thought he would keep the money a little longer just in case.

He couldn't help but wonder how Woody would react if he knew the whole story. He wasn't talking about $15 or $20. There must be thousands of dollars in that box.

Charlie hoped he had fooled Woody into believing the story about the friend. But Charlie knew Woody didn't miss much.

"I'm tired of this stinky motel." Ben Peterson was the tall blond-haired man around 40 years old.

"But we have to sit tight a little longer." Fred Bolsom was shorter and wore a green turtleneck sweater.

"The manager wants to get paid for the room and we ain't got no money," continued Ben.

"We'll just have to stall him," added Fred. "It won't be long before the cops think we left the area. Then we can go back and pick up the money."

"And don't forget the landing, the one with the green shed, two white boats and a dumb beagle," said Ben. "And some pretty good donuts," he joked.

"We won't forget, and pretty soon we'll pick up that pretty white box."

Chapter Five

"This is too long to wait." Ben was anxious as he paced the floor at the motel.

"Will you button up while I'm watching TV!" Fred snapped back.

"Nuts on your TV. I'm sick of sitting around and worrying. I'm going back for that money." With that, Ben's hand hit the knob on the set and the screen went blank.

Fred jumped to his feet.

"Will you calm down? All we need now is to get arrested," barked Fred.

"You're scared of the cops but I'm not," retorted Ben. "You stay low and I'll go pick up the money." He grabbed a jacket and started to move toward the door.

"All right." Fred gave in. "We can both go. But if we get caught, I'll kill ya."

They moved quickly outside, looking around in case they were being watched. The police weren't their only concern, since they didn't intend to pay the motel bill.

Both men climbed into the front seat of their old red Pontiac. Fred sat behind the wheel as he liked to take control of things.

"This is dumb," said Fred. "The cops are looking for two men. We'd be sitting ducks driving around. You get in back on the floor. Put that brown blanket over you."

Ben sneered, but he got out and piled into the back. In a minute the car was heading west down Miller Street.

When they stopped at an intersection, a police car pulled up behind them. Fred gripped the wheel nervously.

"Stay still," he ordered. "A cop is right behind us."

They drove a block, stopped at another corner and started off again. Immediately the startling screech of a siren ripped through the air.

Fred had to think quickly. His first impulse was to floor the accelerator and take off, but he knew he couldn't get away. He pulled over to the side and parked. With a light pat he made sure his pistol was still in his belt.

"What's the problem, officer?" Fred asked as the tall patrolman approached the car window. The nervous crook was trying to act relaxed.

"Your tail light is out and you need to get it fixed."

The officer looked around the car as if he had something else in mind.

"Thanks for telling me. I'll get it fixed right away."

"We're checking a lot of cars today. There has been a bank robbery. The FBI thinks the crooks are still in the area."

"I heard about that. Hope you catch those guys." He tried to sound sincere.

"They shouldn't be hard to find," added the policeman. "There are two of them and we have a pretty good description. The short one has a gold tooth."

Fred tightened his top lip to cover his teeth. Somehow the officer hadn't noticed.

"The second fellow is tall and ugly."

Ben's body jerked under the cover but not enough to be noticed.

"Well, I won't keep you," said the policeman. "Get that tail light fixed and don't pick up any hitchhikers."

"So long." Fred drove away slowly. His hands were trembling and his forehead was cold with sweat. At the first corner he turned left and headed back for the motel.

"I told you it was too dangerous!" yelled Fred. "The countryside is crawling with cops."

"He called me ugly," growled Ben. "He called me ugly."

"No, he didn't," insisted Fred. "The lady at the bank called you ugly." He laughed like an amused ghost.

When they arrived at the motel, Fred parked the car and started to get out. To his surprise an angry elderly man appeared beside his car door.

"I *wondered* if you two were coming back!" The motel manager had his hands on his hips and his face was tight as a drum. "Who *are* you guys? No luggage, no pay, and what is this big ox doing on the floor under a blanket?"

Ben crawled out of the back.

"Well . . . well . . . you see," Fred stuttered. "You see, he's kind of cold."

"Nonsense," interrupted the manager. "It's a nice warm day."

"He . . . he isn't feeling well," Fred insisted. "He's

feverish, so he got in the back under a blanket."

"He doesn't look sick to me." The manager eyed him suspiciously.

"Well, forget that. Where is my money for the room? I'm afraid you guys will sneak away without paying."

"That's another reason we were away this afternoon. My friend had the money, credit cards and everything in his wallet, but he lost it."

"*What*?" The manager wrinkled his brow in protest.

"It's the truth," continued Fred. Ben decided not to say anything for fear they would get their lies mixed up. "We went to look for it this afternoon. If we don't find it today, we will get the cash from our relatives."

"It all sounds funny to me," replied the manager. "How long will you be here?"

"Oh, at least four more days. We have to wait till Ben feels better," answered Fred. He didn't notice the slip of the tongue on Ben's name. The manager did.

Ben took out a white handkerchief and wiped his forehead.

"Remember, I have your license number written down. So don't do anything funny," said the manager.

"Try to trust us. It's a bad time for both of us." With that Fred took Ben's arm and they moved toward their room.

Once inside Fred exploded, "I told you it was too risky to drive around! The cops almost got us and now the manager is keeping his eye peeled. For now we stay put."

His hand hit the television "on" button and Fred

flopped into a chair.

Charlie was going to have to face up to some facts, whether he liked it or not. His conscience kept saying the money wasn't his. He fought its prodding and tried to reason around it. Yet deep inside he knew it was true.

He also knew there was a good possibility the money came from the bank in Easton. Charlie told himself those men had certainly been caught by now. Nevertheless the news of their arrest had not been reported.

"I've got to do something, but what?" Charlie thought to himself. "It's possible the money is stolen. Not likely, of course, but possible. If it is the bank's money, the crooks will probably be coming back for it."

The safest thing to do, he reasoned, would be to move the money and hide it. Sure, if it belonged to someone else he would give it back. But for now he had better find a safer place.

The box hadn't been touched. Its bells and glue were still tight, so Charlie picked it up carefully to avoid making any noise. He didn't want Throckmorton to start barking, though there was little danger of that.

"Collecting eggs?"

The sound of the voice stopped Charlie like a stone. He turned slowly to face her. "Laura, you buzzard," Charlie was furious. "Get away from here or I'll . . . I'll pound you!"

"Kind of jumpy, aren't you?" She stood with her hands on her hips. She always did when she felt sassy.

"You didn't answer my question. Are you collecting eggs?"

"None of your business. Now get out of here before I sic Throckmorton on you."

"What will you give me if I guess what's in your funny-looking box?"

"Beat it, you brat!"

"Is it green?"

Charlie turned as white as the box.

"Maybe," she continued, "it's just a bunch of old pictures of presidents."

Charlie felt his heart skip two beats.

"Oh, don't worry," she assured. "I won't tell anybody. I saw you the first time you found the money. I stood in the bushes and watched you build that dumb trap. Nails and bells." Laura laughed loudly.

"Don't talk so loud." Charlie cautioned her.

"And you think girls are nutty. We know more than you think."

"All right, I'll let you help me, but you have to keep quiet. I'm going to hide the box in the shed. At least for now."

"I wouldn't do that if I were you," said Laura. "Lots of people go in and out of the shed. You'd be smarter to just dig a hole and bury it."

"I was just about to suggest that myself," huffed Charlie.

"What if you forget where you buried it?" asked Laura.

"I'll make a marker and a map," said Charlie.

Charlie got paper, a pencil, and bread bags from the house and picked up a shovel. Laura measured off fifteen feet from the shed and ten feet from the weeping willow tree. Bushes hid their spot from sight of the house. While Laura drew the map, Charlie dug a hole. She liked to draw pictures. The water front was drawn neatly, the shed was a perfect square and the weeping willow had long branches hanging to the ground. A perfect X marked the spot where Charlie was digging.

In ten minutes the money was removed from the box and stuffed into bags, and the loot was buried.

"People can see a freshly dug hole," Laura pointed out.

"I know that," Charlie snapped. He didn't want her to know he appreciated her help. "I'll put this old board on the spot."

Now everything was set—everything except a place to hide the map. Laura and Charlie looked around without saying anything. It would have to be waterproof and completely safe.

Charlie's eyes suddenly fell on a pile of oyster shells near the picnic table.

"I wonder," he said out loud, "about those shells."

"That's it," Laura joined in, "put the map in an oyster shell."

"And glue it shut again," added Charlie.

"And make a red dot on it to mark the shell," said Laura.

"Terrific. No one will find it there." Charlie's eyes were bright.

After the map was securely in place and laid back among the shells, Laura and Charlie sat down at the picnic table.

"If we find out who the money belongs to, we'll give it back," said Laura.

"Of course, but if it doesn't belong to anyone, it's

ours," insisted Charlie. In his mind he could see himself giving it back. At the same time he could see a sparkling new motorcycle.

"But what if it's the robbery money?" asked Laura.

"Not a chance," assured Charlie. "I haven't counted it, but those crooks wouldn't leave their money around in people's backyards."

"I hope you're right. I don't want crooks looking for me."

"Charlie! Charlie!" His mother was calling from the porch. Laura and Charlie ran to the house.

"I have to drive over to Tilghman Island," Mrs. Dean informed them. "Do you want to go with me? Laura can come too."

"Is Pete going?" asked Charlie.

"No, he's next door."

"Sure, we can go," said Charlie nonchalantly.

Laura whispered to him, "Do you think it's okay to leave?"

"Nobody can find the map or the hole."

"What are you two mumbling about?" asked Mrs. Dean.

"Nothing important," answered Charlie. "We're ready to go."

As they drove away from the house, Mrs. Dean began, "I wanted to go early this morning, but it didn't work out."

"Why not?" Laura always tried to join in.

"I was preparing my Sunday school lesson. This week my lesson is about Achan."

"Achan?" Laura couldn't remember him.

"You know," continued Mrs. Dean. "Achan kept

all those things which didn't belong to him. When the Israelites caught him they stoned him to death."

Charlie gulped hard and slouched down into his seat. Laura pointed her finger at Charlie and silently mouthed, "You're going to get stoned, too!"

Charlie clenched his lips and stared straight ahead.

Tilghman Island (pronounced Tillman) is a beautiful spot jutting out into the Chesapeake Bay. Many of its residents catch crabs, dredge oysters and clams for a living. In some cases their fathers and grandfathers and great-grandfathers worked the fishing boats before them.

When the Dean car approached the short drawbridge which connects the mainland and island, it had to stop. Nearly all traffic has to wait at the bridge. Usually, it goes up about every five minutes.

"Some people say it's the world's record," said Charlie leaning forward and sticking his head toward the front seat.

"What's that?" asked Laura.

"This bridge. They say it goes up and down more than any other bridge in the world," replied Charlie.

A small boat was going through. Most bridges wouldn't have to be raised for such a little vessel, but the craft's two flags were too high to go under the Tilghman bridge, so traffic had to sit while the boat passed.

Mrs. Dean drove to the end of the island and parked. She had to see a friend and would soon be back. Charlie and Laura decided to walk around and see the fishing boats. One man remained in his boat, cleaning up his baskets and lines.

"How you doing?" Charlie considered everyone his friend.

"Not bad," the fisherman replied.

"Catching crabs?" asked Charlie.

"They're biting pretty good." The man had a strong Eastern accent. It was thicker than Charlie's and some words were hard to understand.

"How early do you start in the morning?" Charlie figured he had better collect as much information as possible. Later he could unload it on Trooper Hagan or some other friendly ear.

"Usually get up about 3:00 a.m. Of course if I get up at 2:30, I just stay up anyway." The fisherman smiled up at them and his white teeth glowed. "Want a cold drink of water? Climb on down."

Laura and Charlie practically fell over themselves jumping from the wharf. It was a little boat, but by the time Charlie told the story to his friends they would think he was kidnapped by pirates.

"Do you crab all year 'round?" asked Charlie. His computer mind was rolling.

"I usually quit in the fall," said the fisherman. "Some go after them all the way till Christmas."

"What do you do then?" Laura joined in.

"Go after clams. Some fishermen prefer oysters, but not me."

"You mean you go out in winter?" asked Charlie.

"Sure thing. It's cold but not bad. The ice pushes us around once in a while."

"I s'pose you work at this ten or twelve hours a day," remarked Charlie.

"Some times longer," said the fisherman. His smile broke large again across his weather-worn face.

"What do you think about crab farming for the future?" Laura had visited a crab farm on the Eastern Shore and was impressed.

"I doubt it will work. We can't improve on nature. In the cold weather crabs have to stay down 30 feet or they'll freeze. It's hard to take care of them that deep."

"Nature's way seems best," said Charlie.

"I think you're right. If you leave nature alone God seems to keep everything in healthy balance. One year the crabs are plentiful, the next year it's oysters. Somehow it all works out."

After a drink of water the fisherman continued. "A few years ago a large hurricane tore up along the coast. You remember Agnes, don't you? She sent tons of rain and high winds sweeping across the east coast.

"The rivers and Bay were flooded with fresh water from the rain. The rivers up north that feed into the Bay just poured their rainwater down here. That made the crabs fold up, and they haven't produced well for a couple of years."

"And you think this is nature holding things in check?" asked Charlie.

"No doubt in my mind," said the fisherman. "This year I won't make much money, but next year I'll make more. It all comes out even."

Chapter Six

"What're you looking for—pirates?" Kerry asked as he opened the screen door and bounded onto the porch.

Charlie lowered his binoculars. "Oh, just checking out the sea gulls."

He tried to stay cool. Charlie was feeling proud of himself and his secret. Actually, he had taken his father's binoculars to check out his oyster shell. From the back porch he could see the red dot on the shell by the picnic table. This way he could watch his map without getting close to it. He could also see the board covering his hiding place.

Maybe he would grow up to be a private detective or a spy, he thought.

"Did you read about the giant lobster?" Charlie asked.

"What lobster?" The tone of Kerry's voice indicated he didn't trust this Bay watcher.

"Someone caught a lobster that was 3½ feet long," answered Charlie.

"Sure, Charlie, and you've got rocks in your head 4 feet long."

"Pay attention. You'll learn something. It weighed 24 pounds and some scientists think it's 200 years old," continued Charlie.

"Don't tell me—they cut off its leg and counted

the rings."

"Kerry, sometimes I think you have the same I.Q. as wallpaper. It was caught off the coast of Connecticut. A fisherman just lifted his trap and inside was this monster. They kept it for a while but finally decided to drop it back into the ocean. It's swimming around now at about 200 feet."

"Where do you hear all this stuff?" demanded Kerry.

"I read, dummy. You know, words on paper, all lined up in little rows?"

"Very funny. Why don't we do something?" ventured Kerry.

"What little adventure do you care to try?" asked Charlie.

"It's such a nice day, I thought we might go swimming. I even wore my trunks," suggested Kerry.

"Good idea. Here or someplace else?"

"How about Streeter's Curve? We could swim out to the little island."

"Quick thinking for a landlubber," smiled Charlie.

"Landlubber nothing. I'll even race you. Bet you a candy bar I'll win."

"You know better than to bet," added Charlie.

"But this isn't even a gamble. You swim like a brick."

Charlie was eager to go and soon had his trunks on. Streeter's Curve was about a mile away by the shortcut. They cut across a couple of backyards and a field on their way.

This was a favorite spot to swim because of the drop-off. Parts of the Bay area are shallow for hundreds of yards out, but not here. The shoreline has been eaten away at this point, causing a sharp curve.

About one hundred yards into the Bay a tiny island still peeks its head above water. It's around 20 feet across and sometimes disappears when the tide is in. Sailors must be careful to avoid it, so a floating buoy has been placed next to the pesky loner.

"On three," said Kerry as he and Charlie stood by a board for a starting line.

"It seems like half my life begins with 'on three,'" mumbled Charlie.

Kerry's voice rang out, "three," about one second after he started running. They both galloped across the 15 feet of grass and dove into the Bay at the same time.

Both boys were excellent swimmers; they looked like dolphins cutting through the water. Their knowledge of the Bay had taught them to not be afraid. Crabs weren't likely to attack a swimmer; and if they did, their claws could do little damage. Jellyfish could be a problem, but the boys seldom got stung and when they did the sting soon went away.

To these young lads the Bay was home and they were in their glory.

The first ten yards were neck and neck. Three or four people on the shore stopped what they were doing to watch. Kerry started to take a slight lead and Charlie forced himself harder. They were even again after 30 yards.

Now Charlie was beginning to spurt. He moved half a length ahead of Kerry at the 40-yard mark. The young competitors were fighting so hard they didn't notice anything around them.

Suddenly Charlie had a strange feeling. It would

be hard to describe because nothing changed that he could identify. It was an odd sense many people seem to get when they are in trouble.

Charlie knew he was alone.

He stopped and began to dog-paddle. People were shouting from the shore. Though he couldn't hear what they were saying, he had no doubt. Kerry was gone.

Frantically he started to backtrack and look for his partner. Out of the corner of his eye, Charlie could see the spectators pushing a boat into the water.

"Kerry! Kerry!" Charlie screamed.

Like a pop gun a head shot out of the water. It was Kerry and the look on his face made it obvious he was in trouble. He held his side, doubled with pain. Unable to keep afloat Kerry went face forward into the water.

Charlie reached out and pulled him close. By now Kerry had swallowed a large amount of water and was beginning to panic. Kerry turned and grabbed at Charlie.

"Quit it! We'll both drown!" yelled Charlie.

He tried to turn Kerry around so he could hold him under the arms. Kerry reached for Charlie's head and both of them went under.

Charlie came up and threw his arms around Kerry in a headlock. Kerry was still thrashing but now he couldn't reach Charlie. Unable to swim with one arm, Charlie dog-paddled and tried to stay above water.

The boat cut its motor off and coasted close to the two boys. Someone jumped into the water and swam to their side.

"Trooper!" Charlie yelled.

It was Kent Hagan. Kerry calmed down immediately. He explained the terrible pain in his side as Hagan eased him toward the boat.

"Fortunately for Kerry it hadn't ruptured," Mr. Dean's voice seemed comforting as he tried to explain it to Charlie. "His appendix must have come close to breaking, but it held."

Charlie, exhausted, was sitting in his pajamas. He took another drink of hot tea and sank back into his overstuffed chair.

"The pain was terrible. You could see it in his face," added Charlie.

"His parents said the operation went well and the doctors removed the appendix," continued Mr. Dean. "They really appreciated what you did. If Kerry had been alone, he easily could have drowned. You two seem to find more trouble together—but one of you always manages to rescue the other."

"I thought for a while we were both going to go under. If Trooper Hagan hadn't gotten there, it would have been a tough afternoon."

"We'd like to go up and see Kerry Nelson," Charlie told the lady at the information desk.

"When did you turn 12, Charlie?" She knew his entire family.

"Last February, the 10th. And this is Mrs. Alma Nelson, Kerry's grandmother."

The little old lady merely nodded her head without speaking. Her black veil made it impossible to see her face. The old block-shaped hat, broad-shouldered coat and cane made her look her years.

"Room 212. Just 20 minutes for each visitor—and please don't sit on the beds," explained the lady in pink stripes.

Grandmother couldn't walk very fast as they moved toward the elevator, but Charlie was patient. When they finally got on, two more people joined them and Charlie punched the button for the second floor.

"Click. Click." It was an odd noise.

"Click, click." The two other passengers rolled their eyes around trying to find the source of the clicks without turning their heads.

"Click. Click."

All three stared at Grandmother Nelson.

"It's just gum," explained Charlie. "Grandmother loves the mint flavor."

The other two gave an embarrassed smile and looked away.

When the elevator doors slid open the two companions hurried off followed by Charlie and Grandmother.

"Will you throw that gum away?" whispered Charlie, trying to control his voice.

"I just put it in fresh and I'm not throwing it away."

"You throw it away or I'll tell the nurses who Granny really is."

Grandmother lifted her veil. Laura was glaring at Charlie. "Look, sawdust brain—"

Wack—Pop.

Charlie had smacked her sharply across the back; the gum sailed out of her mouth and rolled on the floor.

"You low down—"

Nurses turned their heads to see what the commotion was.

"Grandmother's throat clogs up." Charlie clenched his teeth to keep from laughing.

Laura dropped her veil and moved on down the hall, taking half steps.

When they found 212 they turned briskly into the room and sighed with relief. They had made it.

Quickly they snapped back to attention. Two nurses were bending over Kerry's bed giving him medicine.

"Oh, hi," Charlie blurted out trying to hide his nervousness.

"Hello," answered one of the ladies. "We will be right with you."

In a minute one woman left the room and the other walked over to greet Charlie and Grandmother.

"I don't believe we've met," the lady began.

"Oh, I'm Charlie Dean and this is Grandmother Nelson. She wanted to come up and see poor Kerry."

"How nice of her," replied the lady.

"She doesn't speak a word of English. Her home is in Norway."

"How interesting."

"She just happened to be visiting when Kerry got sick. Naturally she has been concerned."

"Naturally," responded the lady with an understanding tone.

"Well, if you will excuse us, she's anxious to see her little Kerry." Charlie started to move past the lady and Laura curtsied.

"Oh, I forgot." The lady moved directly into their

path. "How impolite of me not to introduce myself."

"Are you the head nurse?" asked Charlie.

"My name is Mrs. Nelson. I'm Kerry's grandmother."

"A-a-a-a-a-h!" howled Laura as she swung around and shot out the door.

"This isn't my fault," blubbered Charlie as he edged toward the door. "That's who she told me she was."

Charlie bolted down the hall and turned at the staircase, chasing Laura.

Everyone in the hall stopped to stare at the running grandmother.

Charlie and Laura escaped through the side exit which led directly to the street. Laura didn't care to parade through the hospital lobby again. By now she was carrying her coat, veil and box hat. Charlie walked briskly to keep up with her.

"You've got to be the dumbest boy in the western half of the world." Laura's words spit out like pistol shots. " 'We'll dress you up like Grandma Nelson,' " she mimicked in a nasal tone.

"How was I to know Grandmother Nelson was here?" whined Charlie. Laura marched on.

"Hey, I'm sorry." Charlie caught her arm and held on. "Maybe it was a dumb idea. I suppose wanting to cheer up Kerry isn't a good enough reason to tell lies to get in." Laura stopped and faced him. "Look, I've got a dollar, what say I buy you a coke and we become friends again?"

Laura looked at him suspiciously. "Are you puttin' me on?"

"No joke," Charlie continued.

"All right, but if you tell anyone you bought me a coke, I'll brain you."

They found a restaurant just one block away and piled into a booth in the back. Neither was anxious to have anyone see them together; although Laura was a little excited.

"Coke or Dr. Pepper?" Charlie asked. "And remember it's on me."

"I hope you won't mind but I brought some money along, and I'm hungry. It's been a lot of evening; I think I'll get something to eat," said Laura.

"No problem, but remember the coke is on me."

Laura wanted a large hamburger, tater tots and a sundae.

"Why don't you get something, too? I've got five dollars. Come on. It'll show we're still friends."

Charlie was never strong-willed when it came to food. "Well, if it will make you feel better. But just a hamburger. Oh, and, uh, fries."

"Fair enough. But you order, after all I'm a lady."

Charlie was winning again. Laura not only wasn't angry, but he was getting free food out of the deal.

"How did your mother ever agree to loan you the coat, veil and hat?" asked Laura.

"She didn't. I just borrowed them, but I'm sure she would have. I'll get them back tonight."

"Is Kerry supposed to be in the hospital long?" asked Laura.

"Probably two weeks. An appendix operation is usually routine but this one is different. When it gets this bad the swelling is slow to go down and they have to be careful to look for infection." Charlie didn't know the first thing about it, but that never stopped him from talking.

"How do you know so much, Charlie?"

"I read a lot and I'm what you call a fast study. When I hear things they have a way of sticking."

"There is a lot of truth to that," Laura agreed. "Excuse me a moment." And she moved toward the restrooms in the back of the restaurant.

Charlie sat alone and smiled. He thought he might tell her about ocean depths and submarines when she came back. Most people didn't know much about either.

The food soon came and it was steaming hot. Charlie poured ketchup on his fries and then added mustard to his burger.

Tony, a friend from school, stopped by the booth and chatted for a few minutes and then moved on. Charlie couldn't decide whether to wait for Laura or go ahead and eat.

"Why not," he thought, "she's only a girl. Who else could take 15 minutes in the restroom?" He picked up his burger and started in. After his burger Charlie headed into his fries. A few minutes later he downed his coke.

"Twenty-five minutes?" Charlie thought. "This is ridiculous." He stole a few of her tater tots.

When his patience was completely exhausted, Charlie decided to inch his way back toward the Ladies' Room. He wasn't sure what he would do, but Charlie couldn't sit still much longer. Besides, what if Laura had fainted or something?

He arrived at the door to the Ladies' Room faster than he expected. Charlie knew he couldn't just stand there; other people in the restaurant would start staring at him.

Because he had to do *something*, Charlie knocked

quickly on the restroom door. No one looked around but he was sure his face was watermelon red. Embarrassed, he knocked one more time.

The door opened. A tall, dark-haired lady looked down at him. "Yes?" she said in the most chilling tones.

Charlie wanted to die. "Well, I was just . . . passing by."

"Weirdo," she grumped as she slammed the door.

Charlie stomped back to his table furiously.

"When I get Laura I'll strangle her," he muttered to himself.

He whisked up his grandmother's clothes. Then, like a dart he shot toward the front door.

"Hey, fellah." A voice shouted from behind the counter. "Aren't you forgetting something?"

"I think I've got all the clothes," Charlie said sheepishly.

"What about the bill? You owe $3.65."

"But you don't understand! That girl ordered them—I've only got a buck."

"I heard you order them myself," barked the husky man. "You trying to rip me off?"

"Can I call my parents?" asked Charlie weakly. He thought, "When I get done with Laura she'll only be 2-1/2 feet tall."

Chapter Seven

"If you want to stay, all right," said Fred, tossing a paper cup into the trash basket. His body unraveled as he stood up.

"And just how do we do it?" asked Ben sarcastically as he checked the pistol in his belt. Automatically he buttoned his sport coat. "That squirrelly manager is waiting and watching. The minute we walk to our car he'll call the cops."

"We've got guns, let's take him with us!" Fred thought he had struck a great idea.

"Sure, then we get busted for kidnapping and still can't get our money," Ben objected.

"Then what?" asked a dejected Fred.

"I might have it," said Ben slowly. "We could go through the motel and sneak out the back. Then we can circle through the bushes and come out next to our car. If we're careful, the manager won't see us until we're gone."

"Now you're starting to think."

Fred flipped the light off as Ben cautiously opened the door. There was no one in the hall so they left the room quickly. Each man looked around as they walked. They didn't know what they would do if the manager came.

Bang! Clang! Fred stumbled over the steel trash can in the hall and fell to one knee. Ben grabbed the tumbling container.

"S-h-h-h, you clod," scolded Ben.

"What was that?" A more than slightly heavy lady asked as she stepped out from a room. She was dressed in a gray exercise suit. Another woman stood by her side.

"It was nothing, lady. My friend just tripped."

"Why, don't tell me," the lady's eyes opened like a startled owl. "You must be Mr. Johnson," she said gleefully.

"Mr. Johnson . . ." Ben looked puzzled.

"They told us you had curly hair," she went on.

"Look, ma'am—"

"The ladies are all ready, waiting, and I might add, eager!"

"I think you've got the wrong—"

"Look," Fred interrupted. A man stopped at the pop machine down the hall. "It's the manager." Fred turned to the ladies.

"You are clever to recognize Mr. Johnson. We weren't sure we had the right room." Grabbing Ben by the arm he pushed his partner into the large conference room.

Ben started to object but realized he had little choice.

"Ladies, ladies!" She blew her whistle, scaring both of her puzzled guests. The fifteen women turned and smiled enthusiastically.

"Mr. Johnson has arrived," she continued. "May we call you by your nickname, Bruno?" A slight blush swept across her face.

"You bet—Bruno." Ben tried not to look bewildered.

"My name is Alice. The ladies of the Parkside Exercise and Garden Club are all yours, Bruno."

The ladies all applauded politely.

"I'll sit over here to the side, Bruno." Fred cast an exaggerated smile to Ben and moved over. Ben promised himself he would get Fred for this.

"We forgot to sing our theme for Bruno," Alice chimed. "All together, girls.

"O—h, We all stay fit
    We bend and sit
    We make our tummies flat.

"We stretch our backs
    Do Jumping Jacks
    We chase away the fat."

"That's lovely, ladies." Ben forced a smile, handing his coat to Fred. His pistol was stuck inside.

"As you probably know, my exercises are a little different than most. Let's do the . . . uh . . . the uh . . . the pelican hop. Yes, the pelican hop. This is the same exercise I taught to Queen Elizabeth. She lost 20 pounds doing the pelican hop.

"Everyone up on one leg. Fold your arms under like pelican wings. Now lift your head up and stare at the ceiling. This will help stretch those neck muscles and tighten up those chins. Let's hop. Start hopping. Don't look down. Just hop."

Obediently the ladies flapped their arms and jumped around on one leg.

"Don't look down."

Ben waved his hand at Fred motioning for him to follow. They moved swiftly toward the door while the ladies continued their modern exercise.

Fred and Ben took one step outside into the hall and whirled back into the conference room. Less than ten feet away the manager was talking to a cleaning lady. They were trapped.

"How are we doing, Bruno?" shouted Alice.

"Great!"

"O—h," Alice started to sing and the others joined in as they hopped.

"We all stay fit
 We bend and sit
 We make our tummies flat.

"We stretch our backs
 Do Jumping Jacks
 We chase away the fat."

"That's enough," commanded Ben.

He whispered to Fred, "What am I going to do?"

"I don't know, but you better keep doing it, Bruno."

"All right, ladies," Ben continued. "Let's tighten up that arm flesh. Everybody pick a partner. Now press your hands against the palms of your partner's. Lean toward each other and start to move your feet backwards. Rest your weight on each other's hands.

"Ready? Start to back up. Lean forward. Move your feet backward. Can you feel those muscles tighten?"

"Yes, yes," several replied.

"When you go back as far as you can, hold your position."

A muscular man walked into the room and Fred quickly headed him off.

"Hello," the visitor said, "I'm Bruno Johnson.

This must be the Parkside Exercise and Garden Club. I'm sorry I'm late."

"Oh, no!" Fred tried to think fast. "This is the Lynchburg Exercise Club. Parkside meets in room 84."

"So sorry. Thank you." The real Bruno strode down the hall.

"Think of something!" Fred whispered to Ben. "I figure we got about three minutes to get out of here."

"That's wonderful, ladies. Now let's sit on the floor," announced Ben.

"O—h," sang out Alice and all joined in.

"We all stay fit
We bend and sit
We make our tummies flat.

"We stretch our backs
Do Jumping Jacks
We chase away the fat."

"Sit Indian style. Fold your legs. Let's move quickly," shouted Ben. The ladies scurried like kittens to a saucer.

"Hold your face in your hands and close your eyes. This will get rid of your face fa . . . I mean flesh. Start smacking your face. Don't open your eyes. Give a soft Indian call."

The ladies began babbling a strange collection of sounds.

"Keep smacking. Don't open your eyes. I can't hear your chant." Each lady was smacking her face with increased strength.

Ben and Fred shot through the doorway. To their left they could see the real Bruno talking to the manager. Without slowing they sped down the other hall and outside.

At the Dean home Charlie was trying to get the lawnmower running. Each time he pulled the cord it merely snapped back. Not one sputter or putt.

"Can't even start a mower," a mocking voice rang out.

Charlie didn't have to look up to know who it was.

"Don't even get near me," barked Charlie.

"It isn't my fault if girls are superior to boys," said Laura haughtily.

"That restaurant man thinks I'm a crook because of you," replied Charlie.

"Well, you are a crook."

"You better get out of here," warned Charlie. "I'll chase you with this mower."

"How can you chase me?" teased Laura. "You can't even start it."

Charlie was fuming. He jerked at the starter cord harder than ever. He would like nothing more than to chase her around the yard with the mower. The machine sat like a stone.

"I think it's only fair to tell you I'm not taking any of the money," explained Laura.

"Quiet, will you?" Charlie's face twisted as if in pain. "You want everybody to know?"

"Right now I don't care," she continued. "I'm not touching stolen goods."

"Laura, you don't know it's stolen."

"Who are you kidding? I suppose you think the Red Cross dropped it off for you? Maybe it's a special gift from the DuPonts."

"Laura, I don't care what you think. Get out of my life."

"Aren't you going to ask me why I'm not taking any?" Laura asked.

"I have a feeling you're going to tell me," replied Charlie.

"My mom taped a new memory verse on the 'frigerator yesterday," she continued undisturbed. "And it was Proverbs 11:1—just for you, Charlie Dean. Do you know it?"

"Nope."

" 'The Lord hates cheating and delights in honesty.' "

"This is not cheating," insisted Charlie and he took another big yank on the rope.

"Then why don't you tell your parents?" demanded Laura. "Charlie, you are a faker. I don't think you really believe this is honest."

"I do, too. It isn't as if I was going to use it all for myself. Sure, I want a bigger bike, but I'll give the rest of it away. Maybe a thousand dollars to the kidney foundation, or for an orphan, or maybe missions. I might give even more since *you* don't want any."

"It will only lead to trouble. Someone will come looking for that money," Laura pushed.

"Maybe and maybe not."

"I read in the paper about a boy in New York who found $500. He gave it back and the owner gave him a $50 reward. I bet you'd get a reward, too."

"You worry too much." He pulled the cord again.

"You don't worry enough," she snapped back.

"Buzz off."

"Be an idiot. But inside you know better. Remember the story your mother studied for her Sunday school class? Achan did exactly what you're doing. He took things that weren't his and kept them. They stoned him to death."

"When you get done, are you going to sing a hymn?"

"Okay. I wipe my hands of this mess." With gigantic gestures she brushed her hands across each other. "You're in this alone."

Laura walked a few yards away.

"One last word of wisdom." She sounded serious.

"By all means," replied Charlie sarcastically.

"You might do better with a spark plug."

Charlie looked down at the empty hole where a plug was meant to go. Furiously he kicked his foot against the machine's steel side.

"Oh-h-h!" He grabbed his injured foot and danced around on one leg.

Charlie was still hobbling when his father came out.

"Here is that spark plug I told you was on the porch," said Mr. Dean holding a package in one hand and a wrench in the other.

In a minute Charlie was down on one knee and putting the plug in.

"Dad, what would you do? Just suppose you found a quarter and you didn't know who it belonged to. Would you hand it over to the police or just pocket it?"

"Well, I doubt I would take a quarter to the police station," Mr. Dean said.

"That's just what I thought."

"Don't tell me that you found a quarter."

"Not exactly," Charlie replied. "Promise me something, Dad."

"I'll try."

"You won't ever believe Laura, will you?" asked Charlie.

"I think I have this strange conversation figured out. You found a quarter and it belongs to Laura."

"No, but it is something like that," answered Charlie.

"Even though I wouldn't take it to the police station, I would try to find out whom it belonged to." Mr. Dean would have dropped the subject, but he sensed there was more to it than Charlie was saying.

"That's okay, Dad. It was nothing." Charlie didn't want to hear too much.

"I'd ask around. Check with a few friends. If I didn't try, it would be sort of like stealing, and that would be breaking one of God's commandments."

Charlie pulled the cord and the mower barked to life immediately. He pushed it away from his dad, glad the machine had started.

As Charlie marched across the yard, a thousand thoughts kept running around in his mind. He was sure he was no thief. Other people had found money. Jesus wasn't against money; He even had a treasurer for the disciples. If he told the police, everybody would probably get a little part of it. Why can't life be simple, he thought.

After two hours, Charlie finished and parked himself on a bench. The mower sat silently at his feet. He looked down at the lettering on the side. It was made by U.S. Steel. For a minute he thought he could see the second "e" turn into an "a."

"It worked better with a spark plug, didn't it?" The voice came from behind him.

"You would work better with a brain." Charlie didn't think he needed more of Laura.

"I bet I know what you thought when you first heard my voice." She still stood behind Charlie.

"Yeah, I thought the ghost of Frankenstein had come."

"You big pretender. You thought you had been visited by an angel and you know it," Laura teased.

"Please don't talk in my yard; you'll kill the trees," Charlie sounded grim.

"Despite your hard shell I have decided to accept your apology."

"My apology?"

"Yes. I realize boys have difficulty being tender, so I will make it easy for you," added Laura. "I am going to volunteer to go with you to the police."

"Get out of my life," growled Charlie.

"Just the opposite. You need me. You won't know how to explain this little episode to the police. However, I'll help you smooth over the rough spots."

"Who do you think you are, Mrs. Perry Mason?"

"Look at me as the angel of your conscience. A shining light in your foggy thinking. A lighthouse in the rocky bay of your shallow mind." Laura spoke dreamily and with great gestures.

"If you go near a police station, they'll put you in a padded cell." Charlie pointed directly at the unmoving Laura.

"Why don't you face the facts? No Christian takes money which isn't his and sleeps well."

"But you forget it's mine. Possession is nine-tenths of the law," insisted Charlie.

"You know in the back of your confused little brain the money isn't yours. It probably belongs to the bank in Easton. You also know that when the robbers come, they are probably going to put black and blue marks all over your cardboard head."

"I get it," said Charlie. "You plan on going to the station with me and collecting half the reward."

"Think anything you want. You still come out of this as a fool," Laura answered. "What would you do if I just happen to mention this to Trooper Hagan?"

"You wouldn't dare," snorted Charlie. "You know I'd get you back one way or another."

"That's your whole problem. You're selfish," Laura accused. "You're just looking out for yourself. This money is turning you into an even worse monster. You're willing to lie, cheat, hurt people. You don't care what people say or what God says. I hope the money gives you leprosy."

Charlie's brother, Pete, came bounding out the back door.

"Why don't you ask Pete?" Laura called loudly.

"You just cool it!" Charlie shot to his feet.

"Ask me what?" wondered Pete.

"Forget it," snapped Charlie.

"What do you know about little green things, Pete?" asked Laura.

"Yeah, like frogs," barked Charlie.

"I think I'm missing something," said Pete.

"You still have more sense than your stupid brother," insisted Laura.

"Your mother must be calling you, Mrs. Perry

Mason," Charlie insulted again.

"It's my privilege to escape from a maniac like you."

"Don't go," said Pete. "Dad offered to take us out water skiing. He even takes girls."

Mr. Dean came down the back stairs carrying a pair of long skiis. He was dressed in a bathing suit and a white terry shirt.

"Run home and get your bathing suit, Laura," Mr. Dean told her. "We can get an hour or so in."

"She has a cold," said Charlie.

"Quite the contrary, Mr. Dean. I never felt better. I'd love to go skiing. I'll run and get my suit. Oh, while I'm gone, Charlie has something he would like to tell you."

Charlie's face turned red as a steamed crab.

"Don't pay any attention to her," Charlie told his dad. "The salt water is corroding her brain."

"Charlie," Mr. Dean instructed, "get that old wooden paddle. We can use it to push off."

Charlie sauntered toward the faded boat and looked around for the paddle in the high grass. He spotted it in a pile of tall weeds and rocks. Somehow he remembered he was supposed to cut the grass here but he hadn't. The mower couldn't go among the rocks and he hated to use a sickle.

Charlie grabbed the handle and lifted.

"Hiss, hiss."

Charlie jerked back and dropped the paddle.

"Dad! It's a water moccasin!"

In the bare spot among the rocks, a hazel brown snake was coiled into a circle. Its long neck was stuck straight up, ready to strike. The reptile's wide open mouth gave it an ugly look. Charlie quickly retreated.

Mr. Dean ran to his side.

"It's a water moccasin," Charlie repeated.

"I doubt that, Charlie. He looks more like a copperhead."

"You better make that a 'she.' Look at those tiny babies," Charlie added.

There were eight newborn snakes wiggling on the ground. The stout three-foot mother was making sure no one got close.

"Look at the top of her head," Mr. Dean told Charlie. "The copper color will usually tell you the difference. People think they see water moccasins, but most of the time they see copperheads.

"They're poisonous, aren't they?" Charlie had found a stick and was ready to defend himself.

"You bet. But not as poisonous as many people think. Once in a great while someone might die, but almost never an adult."

"Well, I don't want her biting me," stated Charlie. He pushed his stick toward the copperhead as if he were holding a sword.

"It would hurt all right. I saw a copperhead bite your uncle. His hand puffed up and changed to an ugly color, but he made it."

"Look at that tail shake," Charlie said loudly.

"Yeah, maybe she thinks she's related to a rattler. There's no noise but that tail sure does a dance."

"Want me to finish her off?" Charlie picked up a heavy rock. Before he could lift it above his head his dad touched his arm.

"Don't do that," Mr. Dean warned him.

"Boy, if Mom heard you say that," Charlie

dropped his rock. "She's scared to death of them."

"They don't want people around anymore than we want them."

"But they bite people," Charlie insisted.

"Probably more than any other snake in America. They also do plenty of good," asserted Mr. Dean. "They eat more rats than cats do."

"She isn't even trying to get away. Just sits there and hisses."

"No doubt she would like to run, but she probably doesn't want to leave her babies. Why don't we put that old paddle over them again? It won't be long before her family moves away."

Mr. Dean placed the oar gently over the copperheads. The snake made a couple more hisses, then lay down.

"You don't have to tell your mother about this."

"I wouldn't dare."

"Sorry I'm late!" Laura was running across the backyard in her bathing suit. "I had to look over my brochure from the Coast Guard."

"The Coast Guard?" Charlie sounded confused.

"I just might go to the Coast Guard Academy," Laura went on.

"You can't be serious," he added.

"Never more."

"Cape May isn't far away," said Mr. Dean. "But you have plenty of time before deciding."

"Still, I might send away for an application. Bet I can get a commission."

"Women in the Coast Guard?" Charlie said with disgust. "Next they'll want to vote."

"And some day I'll catch you on the high seas:

'Halt, Charlie Dean, or I'll blow a hole in your starboard stern.' "

"Starboard stern?"

"Well, whatever." Laura shrugged. "I can learn all those terms later."

"They aren't going to put women on boats with men," Charlie tried to discourage her.

"Indeed," she demanded. "They're on vessels now. That shows you what landlubbers know."

"They won't let *you* in, especially after they see how you water ski."

Mrs. Dean called to them from the porch. A man from the canning factory wanted to talk to Mr. Dean.

"I hope this doesn't take too long," he commented as he jogged toward the house. "I'll be back as soon as I can."

Chapter Eight

"You watch the car and I'll go down and pick up the money," Ben ordered Fred.

"I have a better idea. You watch the car and *I'll* get the money, Bruno," Fred countered.

"Look, if you call me Bruno again, I'm going to bust your head," snarled Ben. "We can go and get it together. Just lift your fat feet."

The two crooks sneaked as quietly as they could through the hedges and into the Dean backyard. They heard a door slam. No one was in the yard.

"Right here," said Ben in a loud whisper. "We put the bait box under this wooden boat."

Fred reached down and felt around. His smile collapsed like a punctured balloon.

"It ain't here!"

"What do you mean it ain't there?" demanded Ben.

"It ain't here." Fred's voice rose as he flailed his hands around frantically.

Ben dropped to his knees and tore into the grass looking for the box. Both men were thrashing around when they heard a door slam.

"Quick, under here!" Ben commanded.

Without a word they crawled under the boat and lay flat on their stomachs in the tall grass. Charlie had come out of the house.

Throckmorton shook his large ears and trotted to the side of the old boat. The beagle stood there staring at his two visitors.

"S-h-h, nice boy," whispered Ben. "Don't bark, old boy. S-h-h."

"We'll give you a bone or a cat to chase," Fred added.

"Throckmorton!" Charlie shouted, "Throckmorton! Here boy." He was carrying a food dish.

"Scram! Scram!" Ben tried to get the hound to leave. "We don't want that boy over here. Beat it!"

Throckmorton suddenly lunged away at a gallop toward Charlie. Eating was the only thing that got much enthusiasm out of the sleepy beagle.

"Eat up, Throckmorton," said Charlie. "Would you like to go water skiing with us? I bet you would. I can see you with your legs spread out on four big skis. You'd hit those waves and just fly.

"I don't know when Dad's going to finish with that phone call."

Throckmorton devoured his meal without raising his head.

"Boy!" Charlie continued. "You aren't much to talk to today."

He went back into the house.

Ben and Fred scurried out from under the boat. "Let's look around—and make it fast," said Fred.

They searched behind trees and the large red bench. They looked along the short shoreline. There were so many tall weeds by the water it would be hard to find anything.

They had no time to lose. Someone could come charging out the back door any minute. Ben stepped on a board on the ground. He had no reason to pick it up.

"The box is no place," Ben said disgustedly. "Some crook stole it."

"Here," said an enthused Fred. "I found it!"

Wedged between some rocks on the beach was their white bait box. Fred picked up the container and suddenly threw it down in disgust.

"Ain't no money in it. Just a bunch of nails in the top," said Fred bewilderedly.

"It looks like some kid had the box. Maybe he has our money, too." Ben was angry.

"We better get out of here," insisted Fred. "They've probably told the cops by now."

"Not too quick. I got to think."

The sound of footsteps on the back porch sent both men behind the shed. Ben peeked around the corner to see who it was.

Pete disappeared into the garage and reappeared with a bright red gas can. He then walked out toward the motor boat at the dock.

As he moved past the shed four large hands shot out to grab him. Fred's palm pasted itself on Pete's mouth and the other three pulled him behind the shed.

"Take him inside the shed," ordered Ben.

Quickly they half carried, half dragged Pete. The shed was crowded with tools, sports equipment, and junk.

The crooks could hear the back door slam.

"Grab that red rag and we'll gag him," said Fred. "If he screams we're in hot soup. I can hold him. Get a rope, too."

Ben scooped up the material in a short minute. They tied Pete's hands and feet. Then Fred replaced his large hand with the red rag.

"Make one sound, kid, and we'll shoot you." Ben opened his coat to show his pistol.

"Let's go, Pete!" Charlie called out as he and Mr. Dean came out of the house. "Laura's here and we're ready."

Inside the shed Pete squirmed and tried to talk, but Ben and Fred held him down.

"Where is he?" asked Mr. Dean. "He came out to put gas in the boat. Charlie, check the garage. I'll take the skiis out."

"I'll help you with the life jackets, Mr. Dean," volunteered Laura.

"Pete! Pete!" Charlie called out but he couldn't be found. Charlie walked around to the front of the house but still no Pete.

When Charlie returned to the backyard, Mr. Dean and Laura were standing beside the shed.

"At least Pete got this far." Mr. Dean was staring down at the bright red gasoline can. "He told me he would put gas in the boat. His mind sure does wander."

"Oh, I'll grab the other life jacket. It's in the shed," said Charlie. He took two steps toward the shed door. Fred held Pete tightly. Ben drew his pistol from his belt.

"Don't bother," Mr. Dean interrupted him. "Pete said he might not go. I guess he found something else to catch his interest."

"Yeah, but I might just as well get it while I'm

here." Charlie's hand took hold of the door. Ben raised his pistol.

"Charlie, look at that tuna ship," called Laura. A huge vessel had poked its head around a turn in the bay.

"Man, what a ship," said Charlie as he looked up. His hand let go of the door and he moved toward the water. "I wonder how much water it displaces? Wouldn't you love to sail on that, Dad?"

"I'd be happy right now to get on my own little putt-putt," said Mr. Dean as he picked up the gas can and headed for the pier.

Laura and Charlie followed, forgetting all about the life jacket.

"Now listen, punk," Ben turned immediately to Pete. "We want to know what happened to our money. It was in that bait box. Who has it now?"

"M-m-m-m. M-m-m-m." Pete tried to answer.

"He can't talk," said Fred.

"I know that," barked Ben. "Take that rag off his mouth."

"You scream and you'll be sorry," Fred told Pete as he untied the rag.

"I don't have any idea what you're talking about," Pete blurted out.

Ben smacked him across the face. "I'm in no mood to play with you. If you don't have the money, you know who does. You have about ten seconds to tell us. Fred, count to ten."

"Why me?" Fred sounded insulted.

"Can't you handle it?" asked Ben.

"That's not funny. One . . . two . . . three . . . "

"Where was the money?" asked Pete.

"We told you it was in the bait box," answered Ben.

"One . . . two . . . three . . . "

"Where did you hide the box?"

"It was under the old white boat," said Ben.

"One . . . two . . . three . . . "

"And you looked there?"

"Of course. You think we're stupid?" asked Ben.

"One . . . two . . . three . . . "

"You want me to help you look for the box?"

"We found the box."

"One . . . two . . . three . . . " Fred sounded irritated.

"Then what's the problem?" asked Pete.

"There was no money in it."

"One . . . two . . . three . . . "

"Stop that, you idiot," Ben scolded at Fred.

"You told me to count."

"I told you to count to ten."

"You said to count until he talked. Well, he keeps talking," Fred reasoned.

"Shut up!" Ben rasped.

"Pete! Pete!"

Fred threw his hand across Pete's mouth. Charlie and Laura had come back.

"We're wasting our time," Charlie told her. "He's probably wandered over to Paul's house. He always does that without telling anybody."

A car pulled into the Dean driveway. Laura and Charlie recognized it right away. Trooper Hagan unfolded his lanky frame from his car.

"Hi, Trooper!" Charlie yelled out.

Ben and Fred froze tight as they heard Charlie.

"Want to go water skiing?" Charlie asked as he walked closer to his new friend.

"Thanks, but not this time," he answered. "I was going down to watch the sail boats at St. Michael's and wondered if you wanted to go."

"We're all ready to ski," said Laura.

"How long will you be?" Hagan asked.

"Probably an hour or so," replied Charlie.

"Tell you what. I can stop back then if you really want to go."

"That sounds terrific," said Laura.

"I'm not sure we were talking about girls," Charlie growled.

"Sure," Hagan started to laugh. "I meant both of you. Take your time. My wife is packing sandwiches. I'll go back for them and be here in an hour or so. See you then."

Trooper Hagan drove off.

"I give up on Pete," Charlie announced to Laura. "Let's go to the boat."

Pete's heart sank when he heard the motor on the boat. How was he ever going to get out of this, he wondered.

"We've got to get moving. We weren't counting on a trooper sniffing around," urged Fred.

"Hand me that broom handle," commanded Ben. "A few whacks on this kid's head and he might remember a little better.

Ben took the stick and lifted it above his head.

"All right. All right." Pete pleaded, "I know where the money is."

"Now you're a smart kid," said Fred.

"Where?" asked Ben impatiently.

"If I show you, will you let me go?"

"You bet, kid," Fred reassured.

"Where is it?" demanded Ben.

"How do I know you'll let me go?" Pete stalled.

"We promise," said Fred.

"What good is a crook's promise?"

"Just because I'm a crook doesn't mean I'm dishonest."

"Where's the money, kid?" Ben pushed.

"You won't kidnap me?"

"I said we won't," said Fred.

"Yeah, but you're a crook."

"Forget this. I want the money," Ben insisted.

"Jessie James was a crook but he was honest," Fred explained.

"Did he ever kidnap anyone?"

"I said forget this!" said Ben.

"I don't think he did." Fred looked puzzled.

"If you're going to shoot me anyway, I might as well keep the money."

"We ain't going to shoot you, kid," Ben assured.

"Crooks are like other people. Some of them are good and some of them are bad," Fred added.

"Go ahead and shoot me."

"Nobody's going to shoot you!"

"Billy the Kid shot people. But I don't think he was a crook, was he?" asked Fred.

"Can I get this in writing?"

"What in writing?" Ben wanted to know.

"You mean that Jessie James didn't shoot people?" Fred asked.

"That you won't shoot me."

"This is stupid, kid," said Ben.

"Nobody ever asked us for a note before," explained Fred.

"Then I'll just die and never tell. Maybe my mother will find the loot." Pete puffed out his chest and clinched his eyes shut.

"I think we should give him a note, Ben," said Fred.

"You're going nuts," snapped Ben.

"What's a piece of paper?" shrugged Fred.

"Shut up!" Ben yelled. "Give me a piece of paper." His teeth began to grind.

Fred searched his pockets and finally found some paper. It was their bill from the motel. Ben had a pencil. It took him only a few seconds to write the message.

Pete read it out loud. "We will not shoot you."

"What about kidnapping?" Pete asked.

"All right." Ben took it back, wrote again and gave it to Pete.

"You think I'm crazy, don't you?" asked Pete.

"What now, kid?" Ben looked exasperated.

"You didn't sign it."

"Here, I will." Fred took the paper and pencil. Ben watched impatiently.

"Don't forget your last name. Otherwise it isn't legal." He thrust the paper at Ben. "You too."

Ben grabbed Pete by the shirt.

"That's all, you punk." Ben breathed heavily into Pete's face. "No more notes. No more signatures. No more nothing. You show us the money right now or you've had it."

Pete knew he couldn't stall any longer. He would have to think of something else.

"Get those shovels. I'll show you where I hid it."

Fred took the shovels from the wall.

"Just one shovel," said Ben. "I'll hold onto our little friend."

The trio moved rapidly outside.

"Where to? and make it fast," Fred told Pete.

"See that maple tree?" Pete figured they couldn't stay outside too long so he kept trying to slow them down. Someone had to come this way.

"Count six yards to the west."

Fred paced them off.

"Now ten yards south."

"Hey, this is in the water," Fred objected.

"That's where I put it and it's deep," said Pete.

"My feet are soaked," moaned Fred.

"Dig, you idiot, before we get caught out here."

Fred started shoveling and mumbling to himself. He dug and dug and dug. Water kept filling up his hole and caving the walls in.

"Are you sure it's here?" asked Fred.

"That's it, all right. Six and ten from the tree. It took me a long time to bury it, but it was low tide."

"Hurry up." Ben was too nervous to stand still.

A noise came humming across the water.

"Faster! A boat is coming," shouted Ben.

Fred thrust the long-handled shovel as rapidly as his arms would go.

"Faster, faster. Let's get back in that shed, kid." Ben pushed Pete toward the door.

After ten more strokes, Fred gave up and ran, too.

"Did they see you?" Ben asked.

"I don't think so. I run pretty smooth."

Ben looked to Pete. "If this is a game, you're going

to be sorry, kid."

"It's the right place," Pete assured them. "And don't forget my note."

"What do you think, Ben? We can't stay here. Maybe we had better just take off and forget the money."

"Don't talk. I have to think," said Ben. "I always think of something."

Fred began singing to himself.

"Shut up!" Ben tried to be calm.

"You don't have to yell at me. We're partners."

"I can't think with you going 'da-da-da.'" Ben's eyes were flaming.

"Music is good for you," Fred said sheepishly.

"I've got it," Ben announced. "We sit tight and hope they didn't see us. After they leave we do a little more digging and we'll be gone."

"Sounds good, Ben," said Fred.

"But you had better not be bluffing, little buddy." Ben's voice wasn't friendly. "If you're lying you're going to be terribly sorry." He fingered his pistol as a reminder.

"Don't forget the note you signed," Pete said with a nervous twitch in his voice.

"You better hope that note isn't tacked on your headstone."

The trio could hear the motor boat reach the pier. Fred tied the red rag around Pete's mouth. They waited to see what would happen next.

Pete's mind raced. He knew he would find a way out.

Chapter Nine

"You know who you water ski like?" asked Laura. "Orca the wonder whale."

"You are so clever with words. You can go back to your job now as cheese mold." Charlie moved away from Laura. Four large skiis were stacked on his shoulders.

Mrs. Dean had walked into the backyard and was wiping her hands on her apron.

"Was the water rough?" she asked Charlie.

"Not bad."

"What did you do with Pete?" Mrs. Dean wondered.

"Nothing," said Charlie. "He didn't go. He probably went over to Bensons."

"I was talking to Mrs. Benson. She didn't mention it. Well, better get to my rolls in the oven." Mrs. Dean returned to the house.

Charlie came back to where Laura was sitting on the picnic bench.

Thunk!

"What was that?" asked a startled Laura.

"Sounds like something fell in the shed."

"S-h-h-h," whispered Ben. "They're outside."

Fred had stood up to stretch and stepped into a bucket. His foot was firmly stuck in the metal pail. He started to shake his leg but the bucket held on stubbornly.

Mr. Dean finished tying up the boat and came ashore.

"What in the world does Throckmorton have now?" he asked.

The brown beagle was carrying a white bait box in his teeth. Mr. Dean took the box from Throckmorton.

"It's a wonder he didn't cut himself on all these nails," said Mr. Dean. "Someone really messed this box up."

Charlie held his breath, hoping his father wouldn't ask any questions. Laura jabbed her elbow into Charlie's ribs trying to get him to say something. He ignored her.

Mr. Dean handed the box to Charlie and started toward the house. When he was out of range, Laura spoke.

"You know you're going to get caught, don't you? The police will find the money and you'll go to jail. How do you look in stripes, Charlie?"

"This is none of your business," Charlie told her bluntly.

"You got it," she replied.

"Tomorrow I'm going to take the money to the bank. I'll put it in my dad's account and then tell him what happened. He'll understand and I bet he lets me keep it."

"Bet not."

"What do you know? You're a girl. And besides, don't ask me for a dime of it."

"Don't worry, I won't. I don't want leprosy."

Thunk!

"A noise from the shed again," Charlie said, puzzled.

"There's probably a cat in there," said Laura. "Aren't you going to do something?"

"It's my cat, isn't it?" Charlie spit out.

"You hate cats, don't you?" asked Laura.

"Only *girl* cats." Charlie pushed his scowling face close to hers.

"Sit still," demanded Ben. "You'll have the whole neighborhood in here."

"I can't get it off," Fred said in frustration.

"I should just leave it on you, you bean brain. Here, give me your foot."

Fred stretched his leg out and Ben took a firm grip on the bucket. He pulled. He pulled again. He pulled some more. Ben strained and his face turned strawberry red. The bucket would not give up.

In desperation Ben began to turn the bucket in a circle. Fred's face twisted like taffy. He bit his index finger to stop from screaming.

"Well, if you aren't going to let the cat out of the shed, I will," Laura announced and stood up.

Charlie stood in front of her.

"Girls really are pushy, aren't they?"

"Boys sure are dumb, aren't they?"

"You let me worry about my cat."

"What about the life preservers? They belong in the shed."

"Just let me take care of everything."

"You're weird."

"If you really want to be helpful, you can find the oyster shell where I put the map," Charlie offered.

The job wasn't as easy as Charlie had expected. Many people had walked past the table. Several had sat there. Throckmorton had rummaged through, chasing crickets and frogs. Suddenly all oyster shells looked alike.

"I'm not looking anymore," Laura protested.

"Oh well," Charlie replied. "We don't need that map anyway."

Suddenly he wrinkled his brow as thoughts flashed through his brain. Maybe the crooks had come back. Maybe they had found the map and had taken the money. No. The board didn't look disturbed. What was the noise in the shed? A cat? Possibly. If people were in there, he could be in big trouble quickly.

"Why can't a guy think when he needs to," he thought. He felt trapped. He couldn't pick up the money in daylight. Suppose the crooks were near. If he called the police, he would probably be in hot water no matter what happened. Why can't a guy think?

"Laura, there are only two things in life I hate. I mean really hate," Charlie announced. "I hate baked potatoes and I hate to admit you're right."

"What kind of trick is this?" wondered Laura.

"No trick at all," Charlie insisted. "But there's no time to talk. Do me one big favor. Go inside and call Trooper Hagan at his cabin. Tell him it's important and I need to see him immediately."

"I'm not really your errand girl."

"Do a guy one big favor," Charlie fumed desperately.

Laura's face twisted into a confused frown as she

started to leave. "Tell him to come right over?" she rechecked.

"Right on."

When Charlie was alone he walked to the board he had placed over his hiding place. It hadn't been disturbed. Not a scratch. That was great. If he could keep it just a few more minutes, all this tension would be over.

Charlie moved cautiously toward the shed and looked carefully around it. He walked on his toes to keep quiet.

Laura came out of the Dean house and Charlie trotted over to meet her.

"No one answers," she said.

"Nuts."

"Maybe he's started over here," she reasoned. "He said he was coming."

"Maybe, but I can't take any chances. I've taken too many chances already." Charlie sounded serious.

He looked around the yard and tried to come up with an answer.

"One more favor, Laura."

"How can I resist? You never call me Laura. It's usually 'Beanhead.'"

"Go get the yellow towing rope from the garage," he whispered.

"A towing rope?"

"You'll see it hanging on the wall."

She obediently trekked off.

Charlie kept looking at the shed and glancing up at the driveway. "Where is Hagan?" he said to himself.

When Laura came back they stalked quietly to the shed. Charlie tied one end of the rope to a tree about two feet above the ground. He then walked ten feet away and tied it to another tree.

"I hope Trooper Hagan hurries," he whispered. "Get a sheet off the clothes line."

Laura asked no questions this time. She brought it back quickly.

"Don't you think you should tell your parents?" Laura whispered, frightened for the first time. "We might need a lot of help in a hurry."

"S-h-h-h," Charlie whispered. "I got us into this and I'll have to get us out. Get me that short two-by-four by the boat."

Charlie's eyes didn't leave the shed door. Laura ran after the piece of wood without wasting a second.

"Can you swing that like a club?" Charlie asked.

"Better than any boy."

A car crunched across the gravel driveway. It had a Vermont license plate. Charlie and Laura started waving frantically for Hagan to come. The confused trooper climbed out of his car and hurried toward the shed.

Before Hagan could get there, Charlie whispered to Laura.

"This is it!"

Her eyes widened and she squeezed the board tightly.

"Pete, Pete!" Charlie shouted. "Come quickly! Look at all this money I found! Pete! Pete! Look at this money!"

In two seconds the shed door shot open. Ben and Fred came flying out like eager bats. Ben led the race. His legs hit the rope and he flipped into the air like an aging acrobat. He landed flat on his face and Charlie threw the sheet over him. He immediately went limp.

When Fred saw Ben fall he tried to stop. Fighting for his balance with the bucket on his foot, Fred swayed back and forth.

"A-h-h! A-h-h!" was all he could yell.

Thud! Laura sent her board smashing into his stomach. Fred slumped over like a clam shell. Charlie jumped on Fred and sent him thudding to the ground.

"They're bank robbers, Kent!" Charlie shouted.

Trooper Hagan grabbed Fred's gun. He then took Ben's pistol, but there was nothing to worry about. Ben was unconscious.

An hour later the police were still searching around Dean's backyard looking for clues and asking questions.

Mr. and Mrs. Dean stood with Charlie and Pete. Laura was sitting on the picnic table and Trooper Hagan was still visiting.

"I hope you realize how dumb this was, Charlie," Hagan told him frankly.

"Yeah, I know," said Charlie, hanging his head.

"If they had used their guns when they came out of the shed, this could have been a bloody mess," he continued. "But at least if you weren't wise, you were certainly very brave."

"Ahem!" Laura didn't like being ignored.

"Well, we all know you were the muscles, Laura," the trooper added.

"Sure, but it was my life they were fooling with," Pete interrupted.

"You can say that again!" exclaimed Mr. Dean.

"That's when I really realized what a stupid thing

I had done—when I realized that my being selfish with the money had put Pete in a lot of danger," confessed Charlie.

"How did you know they were in the shed, Charlie?" Mr. Dean asked.

"Pure genius," Charlie kidded. He continued more seriously, "I was worried when I heard the noises in the shed."

"I thought it was a cat," said Laura.

"I was jumpy. I knew the crooks could be around here looking for the money even though I didn't want to admit it."

"But how were you so sure?" Hagan asked. "Or were you just guessing?"

"No, it was more than a guess," Charlie explained. "Something caught my eye. I saw a stick under the shed and it kept moving."

"That was me." Pete took an exaggerated bow. "My hands were tied but I managed to move a stick with my foot. I bet I played with that stick for an hour. Once I gave up on it, but decided to try again."

"Tell the truth, old Pete," said Laura. "Were you scared?"

Pete grinned and nodded his head several times.

"You didn't really think you could keep that money, did you, Charlie?" Mr. Dean asked.

"At first I did. I really did. But then I knew I'd have to give it back," Charlie explained. "But I was scared and I didn't know whether I should talk to Dad, or go right to the police, or what. This must've been the dumbest thing I've ever done. I think I've learned my lesson about being selfish—even though I s'pose I won't be able to get that new bike now."

Laura began to mock Charlie in a nasal tone. " 'I'm going to buy a motorcycle. I'm going to support an orphan. I'm going to give it to missions.' You never talked about giving it back."

"I never talked about it, but it's true. In fact, you did a lot to change my mind," said Charlie. "Especially with that verse, 'The Lord hates cheating and delights in honesty.' "

"If Pete hadn't been kidnapped you'd probably still have that money in your little hiding place." Laura threw her head back and walked away.

"Girls," Charlie said in disgust. "Who needs 'em?"

End

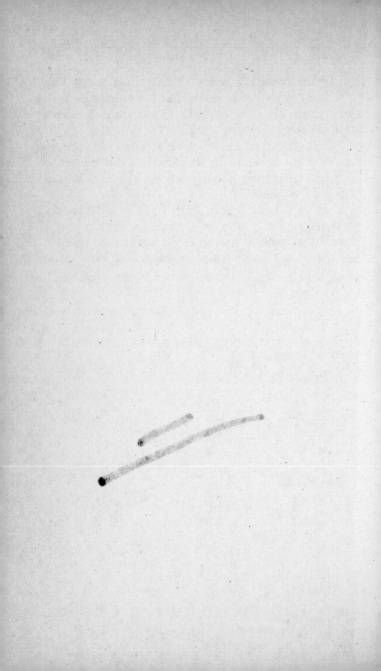